Escape from Sleepy Hollow

Headless in New York

By Kevin Purdy

ISBN: 979-8-9857511-2-3

Visit PurdyBooks.com for information about previous books, upcoming books, free books, and reading/ teaching guides. Follow @PurdyBooks on Twitter (X), Facebook, Instagram and Pinterest.

<u>**Dedication**</u>

This book is for middle school students everywhere. Never stop exploring. Never stop learning. Never stop reading. Books can take you anywhere you want to go and accompany you through life's ups and downs. You are the future, and from what I've seen, the future is very bright.

CHAPTER ONE

Disappearing Legend

Mr. Holland strode from the whiteboard and sank into a squeaky chair. Rolling it backward, he placed his battered hiking boots onto the desktop, scattering papers and books to make room for a pair of oversized feet. "Happy Halloween everyone. We have a special holiday treat today. How many of you have heard of an author named Washington Irving?"

Every hand in the room shot into the air.

Mr. Holland smiled. "Wow! You guys must be literary geniuses. Can any of you name one book that Washington Irving wrote?"

Once again, all hands flew into the air.

Mr. Holland smiled. "I seem to remember one that was called, *"The Legend of..."*

Half the class shouted, *"Sleepy Hollow!"*

"Yep. That book made our little town famous." Mr. Holland set his gaze on a thin, red-headed boy sitting in the front row. "Well, you're in for a treat today, because one of our classmates is going to read *The Legend of Sleepy Hollow* to you. Best of all, he's going to read it from a first edition copy of the book that belongs to his father. Why don't you come on up to the front of the class, Hamlin?"

The class tittered at the formal sounding name of the classmate they knew as 'Hammy.'

Hammy's face reddened to the same shade as his hair. He dug down into his backpack while his teacher provided some final instructions. "Could you please show us the book first? Then remember to speak clearly so they can hear you all the way in back of the room."

Hammy felt around in his pack for the precious old book. It had to be there. He remembered his dad watching him slip it between his laptop and a notebook. He also recalled his father's instructions. "Treat it with kid gloves. That book is worth more than I earn in a month."

Hammy treasured the 200-year-old keepsake that had been passed down from generation to generation in his family. Hammy's parents forbade him from taking the rare publication to his elementary school because they thought he had been too young to be trusted with such a valuable prize. But now that he was in middle school, they decided he was old enough to take it as part of a class assignment.

Except, when Hammy reached into his backpack, he couldn't find the book. He had shown it to his best friends, the Skyler twins, on his way to school. But now it wasn't there.

Hammy's stomach rumbled, from both hunger and nerves, as he frantically dug down to the bottom of the pack with both hands. He began fishing out notebooks and handfuls of snacks until he heard classmates snickering. His face grew warm again.

"Don't worry. They're not laughing at you," Leo Skyler whispered. "Mr. Holland told one of his corny jokes."

Hammy took a deep breath and flashed a weak smile at Leo.

"What's taking so long?" Leo whispered again.

"It's not here." Hammy's voice squeaked as he glanced toward his friend.

"How can it be missing? You showed it to us on the way to school. Did you leave it in your locker?"

"I haven't been to my locker yet." Hammy's voice trembled with a hint of panic.

A third whispered voice joined them. "What's the matter, Hammy? Lose your precious book?" James Dugan wore his usual smirk.

Leo knew that Hammy would take James' question literally, so he replied for his friend. "What's the matter, James? Lose your brain? You could help Hammy find his book, but I doubt you even know what one looks like."

James glared at Leo and was about to reply when Mr. Holland stood up from his desk and walked to the podium. "Is everything okay, Hammy? Did you forget to bring the book?"

Hammy glanced up from his backpack. "It was here this morning, Mr. Holland."

James' voice piped in. "I bet they've got lots of copies of *Sleepy*

Hollow in the library, Mr. Holland. I could go get one for you."

"That's not a good idea, James. You tend to have trouble finding your way back to the classroom once you leave."

The girl sitting behind James started to chuckle but quickly grew silent when he shot her a wicked glare.

"It's okay Hammy. I'm sure everyone in here has heard the story of the Headless Horseman. If you find the book, you can bring it to school on Monday and show it to the class."

"If?" Hammy ignored the part about reading a Halloween book after Halloween. "I have to find the book. It belongs to my dad, and it's really valuable. He'll be mad if I don't bring it home tonight."

"It sounds like someone is in for a rough night." James cackled in Hammy's general direction.

Mr. Holland cast James an irritated glare, then improvised a new lesson to replace Hammy's scheduled read-aloud. "Everyone grab your journals and write an original Halloween poem. Don't forget to be descriptive. Two of you can read yours aloud at the end of class."

Hammy, normally the most creative writer in class, couldn't think of a single word to put in his journal. His mind wandered in a thousand different directions as he tried to figure out what happened to the book… and what would happen to him when his dad found out it was missing.

The bell rang to signal the end of second period. Leo waited for Hammy to stuff all of his snacks back into the pack. And he waited.. and waited…

"How do you fit so much food into one backpack?" Leo's gaze followed Hammy's hands as they placed one item after another into the open mouth of the blue pack. "And why do you need so much food? It's not like we're going to spend a month in the Catskill Mountains. How do you find room for your school supplies with all that other junk in there?"

Hammy ignored Leo's questions and placed the last two fruit strips into his school pack. "How could the book have disappeared? It was in there this morning. You saw it." The two boys walked out of the classroom and into the bustling middle school hallway.

"Are you sure you didn't take it out and show it to someone else here at school?"

Hammy tried to remember exactly what happened once he arrived at school, but his mind felt like it was whirling around in a blender. "I didn't even have time to go to my locker because you and Gwen had to stop on the way here and pull the pants off a scarecrow on Beekman Street."

A new voice joined Hammy and Leo's conversation. "It's a tradition. At least it's not as bad as what the high schoolers do to the scarecrows." Leo's twin sister, Gwen, walked between Leo and Hammy.

"Arr, matey. If it isn't my dear sister the pirate. It seems Hammy has misplaced his father's precious book." Leo enjoyed teasing his sister about the way her dark hair hung down over her right eye like a pirate's patch.

Gwen shot her brother a dirty look, then said, "Maybe it's buried somewhere in that sloppy mess of hair." Gwen tussled the thick mop of wavy brown hair on Leo's head. "Have you ever heard of a comb?"

Leo ducked away from Gwen. "I'm just saying, why would you hide those dreamy blue eyes of yours, little sister?"

"First of all, just because you were born fifteen minutes before me, doesn't make you my big brother."

"And second of all?"

"You're an inch shorter than me, so who's the little one, half-pint?"

They reached Hammy's locker. "Are you sure it isn't in there?" Leo ignored his sister's remark.

"This is the first time I've been to my locker." Hammy twisted the combination on his padlock and was about to open his locker when Leo's voice rang through the hallway.

"Look out Hammy!!"

Hammy felt a tug on his shoulders, then nearly fell over as his school pack was yanked off his back.

CHAPTER TWO
A Grave Proposal

"I hear little Hammy lost his daddy's book." Ely Rudge, a full head taller than both Hammy and Leo began rummaging through the pack. "I bet it's in here somewhere." He pulled out a bag filled with beef jerky and ripped it open.

"I wonder if this could be his book?" Ely chomped down on one of the jerky sticks and kept talking between bites. "Nope. That doesn't taste like a book. It's actually much better."

Without warning, Gwen reached up, grabbed Ely by the ear and gave it a tug, followed by a twist.

Ely let out a yelp that was accompanied by bits of jerky flying from his mouth. "Hey knock it off. Let go." He glared at Leo. "Tell your sister to mellow out."

Leo tried hard not to smile. "What makes you think my sister would listen to me even if I wanted her to *mellow out*?"

Gwen let go of Ely at the same time she yanked the backpack out of his hand. Ely's buddy James joined the group but stayed as far away from Gwen as possible. "It's too bad about your daddy's book, Hamster."

Ely's laugh sounded like a pig snorting. "Nice, James. A nickname for Hammy's nickname."

"Shut up, Ely." James was an equal-opportunity bully who didn't hesitate to bully his fellow bullies. He continued sneering at Hammy.

"I bet you'd do just about anything to find your book, wouldn't you, little…" James peered around to make sure no teachers were within earshot. "… pixie."

It was against the school rules to call sixth-graders pixies. As if that was the worst thing they would be called in a typical middle school day.

"Oh, that's a doozy of an insult, James." Gwen slapped both of her hands over her heart as if she'd been stabbed. "One sixth grader calling another one a pixie. You must have been up all night thinking of that one."

Ely jumped into the fray, forgetting that Gwen had nearly pulled his ear off a moment earlier. "Technically, he's not a sixth grader. He only has to take sixth grade classes again because he didn't pass them last year."

"I said shut your trap." James held up his arm as if he was about to backhand Ely. Then he turned to Hammy. "Today's your lucky day. I might just have an idea where your old *Sleepy Hollow* book is."

"I knew I didn't lose it." Hammy glanced from Leo to Gwen and pointed to James. "He stole it."

"Hey." Ely interrupted. "We both stole it. We're the James Gang and don't forget it."

James glared at Ely. Ever since elementary school, the two bullies had been called *The James Gang*, and their favorite hobby was picking on other students.

"Okay. I'll shut up." Ely took a step away from James, then realized that only placed him closer to Gwen, so he took two more steps away from her.

"I'm not saying I have your stupid book, but I just might be able to help you find it. You know me. Always trying to help those who are down on their luck."

Hammy sent a puzzled expression in the general direction of James and Ely.

Leo shook his head. "In other words, he's saying that he stole your book and he's holding it for ransom until he gets what he wants."

"Ransom is such a harsh word. I think it's more like I'm blackmailing you until I get what I want."

Ely scratched his head. "Are you sure, James? I think blackmailing sounds harsher than ransom."

James hissed at his befuddled friend. "I'll give you three guesses about what I want you to do, Ely."

"Ummm, shut up and…?"

"Shut up. That's all. Just shut up!"

Ely beamed with pride. "I got it on the first guess."

James ignored his annoying friend. "Nobody stole your special little book, Hammy. Who would want it anyway? Maybe someone is just holding onto it. You know, to keep it safe. I bet this school is just crawling with thieves, and your backpack isn't exactly the most secure place to keep valuables like old books and almost-as-old beef jerky. Who knows what could have happened if you set it down on the school steps while you were flirting with little Gwenny here."

Gwen strode toward James. "If one more person calls me little today, they might end up spending a few hours inside the nearest locker."

Hammy stepped between Gwen and James."I wasn't flirting. But I did set my backpack down outside the school for a few minutes. I don't believe that was an invitation for you to swipe my book."

James and Ely weren't nearly as concerned about Hammy's accusation as they were about Gwen's piercing gaze.

"You Three Little Twigs can chit-chat all you want," James whispered, using the nickname he had given to Hammy and the twins back when they were in fourth grade. He cast a wary glance toward Mr. Holland, who had just stuck his head out into the hall. "But if you want your book back, you're going to have to do us a little favor."

"I'll do you a favor." Gwen supplemented her meaningful glare with a clenched fist. Before either the glare or the fist had a chance to sink in, Mr. Holland stepped out of the classroom and strode toward the students. Gwen dropped the fistless arm to her side and did her best to appear innocent, although she had limited experience with that look.

"What are you…" Mr. Holland counted out the number of students standing in front of Hammy's locker, "… five students doing out in the hall when you're supposed to be in class? Gwen and Ely, get into my classroom and the rest of you find your way to wherever you're supposed to be."

James continued his sinister whispering. "If you want your book back, my Hammy friend, you're going to have to earn it. And I know just the time and place. How does spending Halloween night in the Sleepy Hollow Cemetery sound to you and your buddies? We'll meet you at the Headless Horseman Bridge at 4:00 tonight. Don't be late or the book might just go for a swim in the river."

Hammy and Leo watched James disappear down the hallway on his way to the gym. "Was he serious about meeting them at the bridge?" Hammy asked Leo as they prepared to enter their math class.

"Who knows when it comes to those two?" Leo opened the classroom door and turned to Hammy before walking into a room of ogling classmates. "We'll discuss it more at lunch. In the meantime, get ready for a lecture about the importance of being on time for the exciting world of arithmetic."

As expected, Ms. Plummer scolded the two boys for their unforgivable tardiness before handing out a math quiz. She made sure the whole class realized that they would have three fewer minutes to complete the assignment, thanks to their belated classmates.

Hammy hung his head and added this new offense to his basket of shame. Leo smiled and scanned the room as if waiting for applause.

Half way through the quiz, Hammy whispered to Leo. "What are we going to do?"

He had been stewing about the missing book and Sleepy Hollow Cemetery and the Headless Horseman Bridge and the James Gang for the past ten minutes. He had barely been able to answer one question on the imposing quiz that stared menacingly at him from atop his bleak desk.

Leo glanced up at Ms. Plummer who sat grading papers behind her desk. "I'm sure James will tell us more at lunch."

"At lunch? James… at lunch?" Now Hammy had an added worry. James and lunch didn't go together well. Such a combination often ended up with Hammy's lunch on the floor and the entire cafeteria staring at him.

"Leo and Hamlin!" Ms. Plummer was no longer grading papers. "First you two come in late for class. Now you're talking during a quiz. It looks like the three of us may have to discuss this after school today… in detention."

Detention! After school! Hammy's breath grew shallow. Then his throat went dry. It was like a prison sentence. Now he wouldn't be able to meet the James Gang, and they would toss his dad's book in the river, and he would be in trouble with his parents, and Ms. Plummer would—

"Hammy was just asking if he could borrow a pencil. His broke." Leo reached across the aisle and handed Hammy a pencil. "Here you go Hammy. We're sorry if we disturbed your grading Ms. Plummer. We're fine now." Leo scanned the room of gawking sixth graders. "You can all go back to work. Thanks for your concern."

With that, Leo's focus returned to his quiz… as if nothing had happened. The rest of the students went back to work, except for

Hammy. Hammy's hands shook, and he whispered toward the front of the room. "Sorry Ms. Plummer."

The teacher scowled before resuming her task.

CHAPTER THREE
The Plan

Hammy and the twins sat together at lunch, as usual. They did nearly everything together. It was as if they long ago abandoned their separate identities and had become a single three-headed creature.

Hammy barely touched his ample supply of snacks and couldn't wait for lunch to end. This was rather strange since lunch was normally the highlight of his day. On most days, Hammy lived to eat lunch... and dinner and breakfast and snacks. While Hammy worried, Leo kicked a ball to some of his soccer teammates at a nearby table. Nothing ever worried Leo, including pesky lunchroom monitors.

Gwen sat across the table from her brother, making rude gestures in the direction of James Dugan and his bully buddies.

"Don't make them any more mad." Hammy tried hard to communicate with Gwen while not moving his lips or speaking above a whisper.

"Did someone speak?" Gwen's hands began searching around near Hammy, as if she couldn't see him. "Is it Invisible Hammy?" Now her hands found Hammy's face and began groping it. "I can feel him, but I can't see him, and I can barely hear him."

The more Hammy tried to avoid attention, the more Gwen and Leo liked to put him at the center of it.

"Leo. Have you seen Hammy?" Gwen's hands groped the top of Hammy's head, wriggling through his hair while he tried pushing her away.

"He was here a minute ago." Leo joined Gwen, his hands flopping around Hammy's neck and back.

"Cut it out, you two." Hammy stared down at the tabletop while he tried squirming away from the Skyler twins. In his mind, every single person in the cafeteria had stopped eating and focused solely on the freak show at Hammy's table.

"Did you hear something Gwen?" Leo stopped groping and peered around.

"I think it was just the wind," Gwen said. "It couldn't have been Hammy. He disappeared like a ghost, never to be seen again."

Hammy wished it was that simple. He squeezed his eyes shut, as if that would make him vanish until the entire cafeteria stopped staring. He mustered every bit of his courage and glanced up. Not another student in the cavernous room even seemed to realize Hammy's table existed. Everyone else was too engrossed in eating or talking or sneakily looking at their phones which they weren't supposed to even have out of their pockets.

"Isn't this cute?" James strolled up to their table. "Hammy and the twins playing their little lunch-time games. It's just like we're back in elementary school again."

Gwen couldn't resist. "Yeah, James. Elementary School. Or as you like to call it, the happiest ten years of your life."

While James glared at Gwen, Ely blustered his way into the conversation. "It was only six years. Unless you count kindergarten. Then it was seven. Or was it eight, James?"

James' glare transitioned seamlessly from Gwen to Ely. "Ely—"

"I know." Ely hung his head. "Shut my babbling pie hole."

James' glare softened as he turned to Hammy. "We'll see you at the bridge tonight Hamster."

Hammy scanned the lunchroom before asking James, "What if I can't make it. What if my mom says—"

"What if your mommy says no. Wittle Hammy has to stay home and take a nap before going twick-or-tweating?"

As soon as James stopped talking, Ely burst out laughing. He had no idea why except that it sounded funny when James said 'wittle Hammy.'

James didn't laugh. He scowled at Hammy then held up one hand as if holding a book. He pretended to bend over the railing of a bridge and drop the imaginary book into an imaginary river.

Except to Hammy, it wasn't imaginary. It was his dad's book that was being dropped off the Headless Horseman Bridge and into the Pocantico River.

"We'll see you tonight, Hammy, or you'll never see your precious book again." James turned and walked away with Ely following close behind.

Hammy looked as if he was about to cry. The twins recognized this as a sign to stop playing the 'invisible Hammy' game. Silence descended upon the lunch table until Leo swept it away with one simple question. "Are we going to meet them at the bridge?"

Before Hammy could answer, Gwen dove into the conversation head-first. "Are we going to the bridge? What kind of a crazy question is that? Of course we're going to the bridge. How can we push James and his idiotic buddy into the river if we don't go to the bridge?"

Hammy remained silent, staring down at his backpack on the table. On a typical day, his most difficult decision at lunch tended to involve whether to eat both bags of potato chips immediately or save one for after school. Now he had to decide whether to meet a couple of bullies at the Headless Horseman Bridge in order to visit a forbidden cemetery to retrieve his dad's book. In other words, he had to decide if he should plunge headlong into trouble or allow his family's treasure to plunge into the river.

Going into a cemetery after dark wasn't Hammy's favorite way to spend Halloween. He was more of a *read about other people going into spooky cemeteries* kind of guy. It seemed like an adventure when it was described in books. When confronted with actual involvement, it seemed more like a dilemma.

"Maybe we'll just meet them at the bridge, Gwen will give them one of her evil glares, and they'll hand us the book. Simple pimple." Leo's optimism contrasted with Hammy's aura of doom.

"What if it isn't that simple?" Hammy's spirit was proving to be heavier than usual.

"Then I guess we get to visit the cemetery for a while… after dark… on Halloween."

Hammy's lips curled downward into the shape of an upside-down rainbow without all the cheerful colors.

After their final class, Hammy and the twins met on the front steps outside school. "Don't set your backpack down. James and Ely might steal something else out of it." Leo failed in his attempt to cheer Hammy.

"So, what's the plan?" Gwen's enthusiasm contrasted with Hammy's gloom, and she seemed giddy at the prospect of hanging out with bullies in a cemetery.

Ever since lunch, Hammy had been thinking about the upcoming rendezvous. In particular, he was hoping to discover a plan B that was less perilous than the current plan A. "First I have to go home and tell my mom that I'm going to meet some bullies on the Headless Horseman bridge and then take an illegal stroll into a forbidden cemetery."

Gwen shook her head. "Great plan, Hammy. Then your mom will put on her police uniform and go down to the bridge herself. As soon as James sees her, he'll drop the book into the river and make tracks for home."

"My mom's a detective. She doesn't wear a uniform."

"Thanks for the clarification on your mom's work clothes, Hammy, but you may want to make some adjustments to your game plan. So here's what you need to do." Leo had been thinking about their dilemma all afternoon, while he was supposed to be thinking about social studies and science. "You go home and tell your mom that you're going trick-or-treating with us and that you'll be staying overnight at our house."

Hammy looked confused. "How can we go trick-or-treating if we're supposed to meet James at the bridge?"

Leo and Gwen rolled their eyes in unison. "You're not going trick-or-treating, Hammy. You're telling your mom that you're going trick-or-treating."

"But that's a—"

"Don't think of it as a fib. Think of it as a way to make your mom's life less stressful."

"But mom is on duty tonight. What if she sees us at the bridge?"

"Your mom works for the Tarrytown police, right?"

"Yeah."

"We'll be in Sleepy Hollow, right?"

Hammy thought for a moment. "I guess."

Gwen stuck both hands out to her sides, palms up. She looked toward the darkening sky and squinted. "Make sure you pack a rain jacket and hat, too. It's starting to rain."

"Like it does every Halloween," Leo muttered.

"Not every Halloween," Hammy said. "Sometimes it snows."

Gwen glared at Hammy and pointed in the direction of his house. "We don't say the 'S' word on Halloween. Now get home and remember what to tell your mom. We'll meet you by the park at 3:45.

This is going to be a Halloween we'll never forget."

CHAPTER FOUR

Meeting at the Bridge

Hammy slipped his jacket over his sweatshirt and was soothed by the sound of light raindrops tapping on his hood. He and the twins hugged the inside edge of the sidewalk to avoid being drenched by passing cars that zipped through every mud puddle and pothole along the road.

"The next driver that sprays water on me is going to wish they hadn't." Gwen glared at each passing motorist, daring them to splash her.

"You'll have to catch them first," Leo informed her.

"They have to stop sometime."

Hammy had more pressing issues on his mind. "Maybe James and Ely won't be at the bridge. Maybe they already threw Dad's book in the river."

"You don't have to worry about them not showing up." Leo pointed up the road where two familiar figures stood on the old bridge. "I don't think they'd stick around if they didn't have the book."

The three continued walking until they were across the street from the two thugs. James was holding the *Sleepy Hollow* book, making no attempt to shelter it from the rain, much to Hammy's dismay. "He might as well drop it in the river. It's getting wet anyway."

As if James heard Hammy's muttered complaint, he held the book over the edge of the bridge and smiled at the approaching trio. "One false move, and the book goes swimming with the fishies." He hollered, trying to sound like some old-time mafia hitman.

Hammy held his breath as he pictured the book slipping out of

James' hand and plummeting into the water.

Gwen walked up to within inches of James. "You do realize that if you drop that book into the river, you'll be going in after it?"

"Oh I'm so scared." James said, not sounding quite as brave as he intended.

Leo exchanged a withering glare with Ely then added, "Why don't you just hand us Hammy's book? Then you can return to your usual Halloween traditions like stealing candy from little kids."

"We did that last year," Ely said. "This year we get to have fun with you three weasels."

Gwen snarled at Ely. "Weasels have very sharp teeth, you know."

Ely stepped behind James, who continued the conversation. "You don't have to play if you don't want to. And we don't have to give you your book back, either."

"You said you'd give it back if we showed up at the bridge," Hammy said. "We're here, so hand it over."

"We're here, so hand it over." Ely tried his best to mock Hammy but sounded like a Saturday morning cartoon character.

James ignored his sidekick. "If you want your book, you're going to have to earn it. If we were going to hand it over to you, we could have done that at school. Where's the fun in that?"

Gwen stomped up to James so that her nose was only inches from his face. "We wouldn't want to bore you, so how about if I just take the book and send you for a swim?"

James held the book over the edge of the bridge once again.

Hammy's voice rose to one pitch above a squeak. "Let's listen to what James has to say, Gwen." His head motioned for Gwen to move away from the crazy guy with the book.

Gwen stepped away, and James continued. "There's someone in the cemetery who is dying to meet you."

Ely bumbled into the conversation. "I thought everyone in the cemetery already died?"

James ignored his clueless friend. "This person's name may sound familiar to you. She's called the Bronze Lady, and I guess she's got quite a reputation around here."

"Everyone knows who The Bronze Lady is," Leo said. "What does she have to do with us?"

"I'm so glad you asked." James sneered. "You're going to pay her a visit tonight."

Ely jumped in. "Yeah. You're going to sit on her lap, all three of you." His snorting laugh sounded creepier than usual.

"Ummm," Hammy had no idea what they were talking about. "Who is this Bronze Lady, and why is she in the cemetery? And why would we sit on her lap?"

"Hammy, Hammy, Hammy." James shook his head as if in pity. "How could you live in Sleepy Hollow and not know about the Bronze Lady?"

"I don't live in Sleepy Hollow. I live in Tarrytown."

James ignored Hammy. "The Bronze Lady sits in the graveyard and keeps guard over a haunted mausoleum. She wanders through the cemetery at night and searches for creeps like you guys so she can chase you around the tombstones until you're bawling like little lost lambs."

Leo's eyes grew big, and he seemed to be in a trance. "Anyone who sits on her lap will be haunted for the rest of their life. And if you knock on the door of the mausoleum, the spirit of some old Civil War soldier will pop out and scream at you until you wet your pants."

"Bull droppings!!" Gwen chuckled. "I've seen the Bronze Lady. She's only some dumb statue like all the other ones in that place." She nodded toward the cemetery.

"Have you seen her at night?" James asked, his voice somewhere between a whisper and a shout.

"No, I haven't seen her at night." Gwen's voice reflected her irritation. "I don't hang around graveyards at night."

"You mean you *didn't* hang around graveyards at night," James sneered. "Because that's what you're doing tonight. Now one last thing. Hand over your cell phones. We don't want you calling your mommies and daddies when the mean old Bronze Lady scares the snot out of you."

The expression on Leo's face suggested an invitation for James to jump off the bridge. "I don't think that's going to happen anytime soon."

"How about I show you what is going to happen soon?" James once again held the book over the river. "We'll give your shiny new phones back when we give your boring old book back."

Hammy reached into his pocket and withdrew his phone. He flashed a glance at Leo and Gwen, hoping that they would do the same.

The twins handed their phones over to James with Gwen muttering something about where the *boring old book* would end up if she didn't get her *shiny new* phone back.

"How do you know if we sit on the Bronze Lady's lap?" Leo asked. If we had our phones, we could take a picture and show you.

"I'm so glad you asked," James leered. "Since I'm such a swell guy, I've got something to give you in exchange for your phones." He handed a black, plastic box to Hammy. It was the same length and width as his cell phone, but was about three times as thick.

"What is this?" Hammy explored the small plastic gadget, turning it over to inspect each side.

"Don't you even recognize the latest technology when you see it?" Ely drawled. "It's a camera, you idiot."

Ely calling someone an idiot was laughable. Even James had a smirk on his face as he said, "All you have to do is press this thing to take a picture."

He pointed to a round button on top of the camera. "Then you twirl this around with your thumb until it won't go around any more. I want to see a picture of all three of you stooges sitting on the Bronze Lady's lap. I'll give you extra bonus points for a photo of Hammy kissing her on the cheek. They say you'll have nightmares for a month if you do that."

Hammy tried to consider one reason why he would do that, but soon gave up as he twisted the camera around in his hands. "I don't get it. Where do I find the picture after I press the button?"

James shook his head and cast a pitiful glance toward Hammy. He relished the opportunity of being a know-it-all for a change. He was actually more of a know-very-little, but that didn't stop him from gloating.

"This is called a disposable camera. It's too complicated for you to understand."

"In other words, you don't understand it," Gwen scoffed.

"Whatever," James said. "Just take the pictures and give the camera back to me. Once you hand me the camera, I'll hand you the book. And don't try to pull a fast one. If I don't find any Bronze Lady photos, I'll come looking for you. I know where you live."

"I don't think you do know where we live, James," Gwen replied.

"Well, I.. I know where you eat lunch," James stammered.

The threat was lost on Gwen, but Hammy didn't like the sound of it. "Are you sure you'll be here when we come back with the camera?"

"Oh, we'll be here all right. I can't wait to see you three running out of that cemetery bawling like little babies with the Bronze Lady right behind you." James nudged Ely who seemed to be pondering whether he wanted to be anywhere near a runaway statue.

"Now I suggest you start moving. They won't let you into the cemetery after 4:30, and it's pretty close to that time now." James glanced toward his wrist, as if he wore a watch. Then he shot a taunting smile in Hammy's direction.

CHAPTER FIVE

Into the Cemetery

Thick, gray clouds intensified the oncoming darkness of a gloomy Halloween evening. Hammy glimpsed the steeple of Old Dutch Church looming ahead as the trio stepped through the brick and iron entrance at the south gate of Sleepy Hollow Cemetery. No sooner did they cross the forbidding threshold than they were approached by a cemetery guard. Hammy thought it rather strange that a graveyard would have a guard. He couldn't help but wonder if any of the residents had ever tried to escape.

"You can't be in here after 4:30," The guard spoke as if the witching hour was nearly upon them.

Gwen didn't sound the least bit intimidated. "It's okay, sir. We're joining that group in the parking lot for a lamplight tour." She pointed toward a writhing knot of people who were gathered around a tall man in a colonial settler's costume. He was holding a glowing lamp and reminded Hammy of a boat pilot on the River Styx.

"Are your parents in the group?" The guard asked, cocking an eye at the three students.

"Well, of course they are," Gwen shot back without hesitation. "You don't think we'd be going into a cemetery at night without our parents, do you?"

Gwen's ability to fib in such a carefree manner was both a mystery and a concern for Hammy, who was neither fond of lying nor the least bit proficient at it. Gwen, on the other hand, was well practiced at the art of deception. It made no sense to Hammy, but Gwen thoroughly enjoyed stretching the truth until it broke into little bits.

Gwen led the other two toward the milling group of people gathered in the parking lot. The costumed tour guide held a microphone to his mouth and instructed the group, "Let's start gathering on the lawn near the Old Dutch Burying Ground." He pointed in the direction of an old gray church.

Gwen looked around to make sure the guard wasn't still watching them. Then she motioned for Hammy and Leo to follow her as she continued up the narrow cemetery road.

"Do you have any idea where we're going?" Hammy asked Gwen.

Before Gwen had a chance to reply, Leo answered for her. "Our dad is a history freak. You know how you read books all the time?"

"Yeah?" Hammy was trying to figure out the connection between his books and the Sleepy Hollow graveyard.

"Our dad reads cemeteries."

Now Hammy's head began spinning at a faster pace. "You can't read cemeteries."

"Tell our dad that. He comes to this place all the time. Sometimes he brings us. It used to be fun. But after about the fiftieth visit, it lost some of its charm."

"How 'bout you, Hammy?" Gwen asked, still marching in front of the boys. "Have you been in the cemetery before?"

"A couple times, but only during the day. It's weird being here at night." Hammy stopped and looked around, as if he'd lost something. "When my sister graduated from high school a couple years ago, she had her picture taken at the stick bridge. Is that anywhere near here?"

Gwen wore a puzzled expression as if Hammy had just started speaking a foreign language. "What is the stick bridge?"

"I bet he's talking about the Old Horseman Bridge. That's what our dad calls it," Leo explained. "It's down there." Leo pointed toward a thick band of trees that grew along the river banks.

"Why does he call it that?" Hammy asked, struggling to keep up with the Skyler twins.

"He says it looks more like how bridges looked back in the days of Washington Irving."

"In *The Legend of Sleepy Hollow*, the Headless Horseman rode over a wooden bridge." Hammy considered himself an expert on the subject.

Gwen turned around and growled to Hammy and Leo. "Can't you two walk and talk at the same time? Hurry up. And keep an eye out for cemetery guards. As of two minutes ago, we're not supposed to be here. They drive around in their little trucks and golf carts looking for people to harass. If you see their lights, hide behind the nearest tombstone."

"Tombstone?" Hammy groaned.

"Yeah. They're those gray things sticking out of the ground with lots of writing on them."

"I know what a tombstone is," Hammy said. "I just don't like the idea of using them as hiding places."

"Their owners won't mind," Leo said. "At least I assume they won't."

The three walked in silence past stark gray shrines of various sizes from small headstones a bit higher than their knees to massive pillars towering nearly as high as some of the trees. Even during the day, Sleepy Hollow Cemetery was slightly unnerving. At night, it was downright scary.

They only had to duck behind the eerie slabs a couple times before Gwen pointed and said, "I think it's behind that creepy mausoleum."

"She," Leo said, correcting his sister.

"What?" Gwen stopped short, causing Hammy to run into her.

"*She's* behind the creepy mausoleum," Leo clarified. "You said 'it's behind that creepy mausoleum.' I believe the Bronze Lady is a she, not an it."

"But it's a statue, not a real lady. So it's an it, not a she."

Hammy had been listening to these verbal clashes between the Skyler twins for years. They were never all that enjoyable in the best of circumstances. It was somewhat less entertaining in a dark cemetery. "Since I'm going to be sitting on it's lap, I'm going along with Gwen on this one. It's an it. Now please be quiet so we can finish this little assignment and get out of here."

Gwen was a few steps ahead of the others when she came to an abrupt halt and stared straight ahead. Her voice was hushed, for a change. "Yep. This is it."

As the other two rounded the mausoleum, a silver beam of moonlight showed through the otherwise impenetrable clouds beaming down onto the creepiest statue Hammy had ever seen. It was darker than the night, yet the moon's white beams penetrated the blackness to reveal downcast eyes on a somber face.

Hammy instinctively stepped back behind the mausoleum again, as if hiding from the sightless gaze of the statue. He peeked around the corner of the building, fearing the bronze figure would come to life at any moment and chase him through the cemetery.

Gwen chuckled. "I hope you realize you're freaking out about a harmless statue while hiding behind the mausoleum of a dead guy."

Hammy jumped away from the stark gray building and let out a yelp, causing Gwen to clap her hand over her mouth to keep from laughing.

Ignoring his friends, Hammy cautiously walked toward the Bronze Lady. "Why does she have to look so sad?"

"Well, this is a cemetery," Leo said. "And unlike my sister, some people show the proper level of dignity while visiting such a sacred place."

"Hey, you laughed too." Gwen responded. "Besides, being sad is her job. That's why she's here. Some Civil War guy is inside this mausoleum, and his wife wanted a statue to watch over him. I'm not sure why. It's not as if the guy was going anywhere."

"Are you SURE about that?" Leo snuck up behind Hammy and barked in his ear.

Hammy's feet barely touched the ground as he bolted over to where Gwen was standing. He shot Leo a fierce gaze, but it was lost in the dark.

Leo smirked, "I have no idea if the statue was a she or an it, but I know I just scared the she, it out of Hammy.

Gwen tried hard not to laugh."Since you're here," she said to Hammy, "how about if you jump up on her lap and give her a juicy smooch? Leo can take your picture, then we can say goodbye to this lovely place."

"Me?" Hammy whined. "James wants a picture of you guys on her lap too. Since you're so brave, why don't you go first? And I have no intention smooching her," Hammy added.

Leo handed Gwen the camera. "While you two stand here chatting, I'll be the first one to visit our bronze friend." He scampered right up to the base of the statue and clambered up onto the bench beside the Bronze Lady. He looked puny sitting beside her.

Gwen pressed the camera button, and they were all startled by a bright flash, followed by a high-pitched whining sound. Although not loud, it made an eerie noise as it shot off in all directions through the silent grounds of the cemetery.

"You're supposed to sit on top of her lap, not beside it," Gwen said to her brother.

"Fine." Leo grasped ahold of one of the statue's weirdly muscular biceps and crawled up onto her lap, sinking down between her outstretched arms. While Gwen snapped his photo, Leo pointed toward the mausoleum. "Hey! Is that the Civil War general looking out of those big doors?" Leo waved his hand as if greeting one of his soccer buddies.

Hammy inched a little closer to Gwen. "He's kidding, right?"

Gwen ignored Hammy and told her brother to quit clowning around and climb down. She turned to Hammy. "Your turn, little buddy."

"What about you?"

"What about me? I'll go next. I'm the official photographer now. You're my next subject. Hop up on her lap and say cheese." Gwen pointed to where Leo was crawling down.

Hammy discovered a host of reasons for stopping on his way to the Bronze Lady. His shoelaces needed to be tied, his raincoat needed to be zipped up a wee bit more and, of course, he needed to stop for a snack along the way. Gwen reminded him that it was his book they were here to rescue and hinted that she might decide to call this whole mission off if Hammy didn't start moving a little faster than the statue.

Hammy picked up his speed somewhat, but it went from a glacial pace to a snail's pace. When he eventually arrived at the base of the statue he inspected it from bottom to top before mounting a quick scamper up to the lap where he shouted down to Gwen. "Hurry. What are you waiting for? Take the picture. We don't have all night."

Gwen, for her part, became quite particular about getting Hammy in the perfect pose so his mop of red hair didn't cover his hazel eyes. Then, she appeared to have trouble finding the proper button to cause a photo to be taken. Both Hammy and Leo agreed that she'd better speed things up before the sun came up, and Halloween turned into November.

As soon as Hammy saw the camera flash, he bounded down from the statue as if it was on fire. He rushed over to Gwen and retrieved the camera from her. "Okay, it's your turn. Hurry up so we can get out of here."

Gwen mumbled, "Now we're in a hurry." She obviously wasn't the least bit concerned about curses, nightmares or legends as she insisted on striking a dozen poses with the statue. She settled into the Bronze Lady's lap and said, "Okay, this will be the last shot, and then we can leave this lovely place."

"It's about time," Hammy said, preparing to take the final photo. But when he looked through the viewfinder, he noticed that Gwen's expression had transformed from playful to frightful. It was dark, but Hammy could clearly see that Gwen was as stiff as the statue she was sitting on. Her eyes were bulging.

Whatever Gwen had seen, Leo spotted it too, and he let out an uncharacteristic yelp. He started running in the direction of the statue that Gwen was now clambering down from. He reached the statue's base right when Gwen jumped to the ground. Then they both pointed in Hammy's direction, too scared to utter a single word.

Hammy lowered the camera. "Quit clowning around, you two."

Immediately after he spoke, Hammy understood that Gwen and Leo were not joking, for a change. The closer he looked, the more he realized they were dead serious.

"Behind you, Hammy. Run!!!" Leo shouted.

It took every ounce of courage Hammy could muster to turn around and look in the direction the twins were pointing. As soon as he saw what was behind him, he wished he hadn't turned around. He wished he hadn't come into the cemetery on this rainy October night. He wished he had not even gotten out of bed that morning.

CHAPTER SIX

Headless in Sleepy Hollow

Hammy had never seen anything like the gigantic beast that confronted him in Sleepy Hollow Cemetery. Plumes of steam shot out of its flaring nostrils with each snorting breath. The horse's ears loomed larger than life, sticking straight into the air like bat's wings above a pair of fiery blazing eyes.

Hammy stood closer to the mausoleum than the twins, so he could only see the front portion of the midnight black horse. But after the beast took another couple steps forward, a towering rider appeared. The mysterious equestrian was dressed in black clothing. His legs were covered in dark riding pants that crept down over his polished dark boots. A sable cape draped all the way down to the belly of his steed. As if to separate the man's body from his head, a white, ruffled collar encircled his neck and was tucked into the black shirt.

But it wasn't the rider's clothing that caught Hammy's attention and set his hands to shaking. For above the champing black steed and the bizarre clothing, instead of a head, there rested a bright orange, scowling jack-o-lantern ablaze with a yellow glow. Its eyes and nose were the classic triangular shape except, instead of the glowing light beaming out from these openings, it came from underneath the brim of a floppy straw hat that perched atop the pumpkin head.

The horse rose up onto its hind legs, clawing its front legs into the air. Then it stomped toward Hammy, who stood paralyzed with fear. Gwen's scream broke his silent reverie. "Run, Hammy!!!"

The shrill cry shattered Hammy's trance as he spun around and headed toward the Bronze Lady where he thought he would reunite with the twins. But as he drew near the statue, his two friends were lost in the gray mists floating upward from the Pocantico River. He began to turn back toward the mausoleum when Gwen's voice rang out. "Don't look back, Hammy. Run toward the Old Horseman Bridge." Before Hammy could argue, she added, "Or whatever you want to call it."

Hammy needed no further prompting and sprinted faster than he had ever run in his life. The enveloping darkness and uneven terrain made it difficult, and he stumbled several times. Ahead, he saw the faint outlines of two running shapes, and he struggled to catch up with Gwen and Leo.

As if sensing Hammy's dilemma, Leo turned and shouted, "Come on, Hammy. Keep running downhill. Horses can't run as fast downhill."

Gwen's exasperated voice followed. "That's bears, stupid."

Leo didn't bother to argue. He turned and kept running once Hammy began to catch up with them.

"Stay on the road," Leo yelled. "We can run faster on the pavement."

The clip-clop of hoof beats grew louder and closer.

"It sounds like the horse can run faster too," Hammy wheezed.

Gwen apparently hadn't gotten the memo about staying on the roads, and she veered off the asphalt and stumbled over the uneven grass, looking like a slalom skier as she zig-zagged between headstones.

"Where are you going?" Leo shouted.

"If we're looking for the bridge, we'll have to get down to the river. I can't find any roads that run in that direction." Even Gwen was having trouble running over the uneven ground, in the dark.

Hammy followed blindly. As he neared each grave marker, he imagined a rotting hand reaching up from the ground and grabbing him around the ankles to pull him down into the underworld.

Finally after a particularly steep portion, they came to another road. "There it is," Gwen said.

Hammy couldn't see a bridge, but he heard the river.

Gwen discovered a road that headed directly toward the babbling water, and she followed it until it came to the bridge. Even in the dark, Hammy could tell that it was the one he had been to with his sister.

The sharp clip-clop of horse's hooves drowned out the sounds of the river that ran beneath the three wanderers. They were in the middle of a bridge in plain view of anyone with or without a head. Any minute, the Headless Horseman would also be on the bridge, and that would be the end. They were caught in the worst place. In one direction was the Headless Horseman and on either side was a drop-off into the river. The only way left to go was straight ahead, across the bridge.

Unsurprisingly, Gwen took charge. "As soon as we get over the bridge, jump off on the right-hand side."

Hammy had no idea what he would be jumping into. Would it be a long fall onto the many rocks that lined the river? Would it be into the river itself? Maybe it would be into a patch of thorny bramble that would tear his clothes to shreds and scratch his skin to bloody ribbons.

As soon as they got across, just as the hoofbeats grew unbearably loud, Leo shouted, "Jump!!!"

The choices were to face the horseman or jump off into the unknown. Hammy didn't like either option, but he would rather jump into the void, with Leo and Gwen, than face the dreaded Headless Horseman… so he jumped.

It turned out to be a little of everything he feared. He plummeted off a scary drop-off that sent him crashing onto a large, flat rock where he threatened to tumble head-over-heels into the river. In the meantime, he reached out to an overhanging branch to stop himself. Of course the branch was studded with thorns, and it was all Hammy could do to stop himself from crying out in pain.

The Skyler twins were out of sight, one of them behind a rock and the other one hidden in the bushes.

Gwen hissed one word to Hammy. "Hide." Then she added a couple more words. "—you idiot."

Hammy crouched down behind a large boulder so that he could no longer see the road. But he heard the hollow clopping of the horse's hooves as it crossed the bridge they had just been standing on.

Hoofbeats echoed along the riverbed, the hollow sound bouncing from rock to rock and amplified in the ears of three shivering runaways. The horse stopped in the middle of the bridge, as if watching and listening for its young prey.

Through the darkness and mist, Hammy could see his two companions, crouched in their hiding spots, fearful of moving, talking or breathing.

The horse and its freakish rider turned around in the center of the stick bridge and thumped back in the direction from which it had arrived. It seemed to take forever for the thunderous hoofbeats to fade away.

Hammy began shivering uncontrollably from cold, dampness and overwhelming fear. Yet he didn't dare emerge from his hiding place behind the rocks. He peered into the gray surroundings in hopes of spotting his companions, but instead of seeing them, he heard Leo.

"I think it's safe to come out, but don't go up on the road yet. I don't know how far away he ... it is."

The three gathered on a flat spot that was below the road and above the river. They all looked toward the bridge and beyond, hoping not to see the creepy horse or its creepier rider.

For one of the first times in her life, Gwen whispered. "We've got to get out of here. I'm freezing, and it's not getting any warmer."

As if to emphasize Gwen's observation, the light mist turned back into a steady shower. All three of the shivering teens made their way up onto the road and then began crossing the bridge again, wary of any unusual sights or sounds.

Halfway across the bridge, Leo spoke in hushed tones. "If that thing was anywhere near, we would be able to see his glowing head. That's our only advantage. He's easier to spot than we are."

Gwen slowed down so that her friends could hear her. "Follow me." She dove into a thicket of bushes and trees, most of them without their summer foliage and all of them very prickly and scratchy. Hammy and Leo followed, as commanded.

Gwen lay flat on the ground, face down. She turned her head, placed her index finger on her lips and hissed, "Get down and stay down. Don't make a sound and don't move."

The boys followed orders, and hoofbeats passed near them on the road. None of the The Three Little Twigs moved or dared to breathe until the clopping sounds had faded to silence. Then they took a breath but remained still.

Hammy broke the silence. "According to the cemetery rules, we're supposed to stay on the road."

"Really?" Gwen turned to face Hammy. "We're being chased by a guy who is riding a demon horse and has a pumpkin for a head, and you're worried about the cemetery rules?"

Before Gwen could turn Hammy into the headless sixth grader, Leo joined the conversation. "What was that... thing?"

"I'm no expert," Gwen said with a shade of sarcasm in her voice. "But it looked like a horseman who had no head. Have either of you ever heard of anything like that before?"

"Sounds a lot like the Headless Horseman," Hammy exclaimed as Gwen's sarcasm soared above his head.

"Gee, Hammy. That's a great name. From now on, that's what we should call him."

Hammy detected a slight hint of insincerity in Gwen's voice.

"So what are we gonna do? If we try to get out of here, we'll have to follow the headless dude. Seems like a poor choice," Leo said.

"There's another way." Gwen answered her brother. "Don't you remember the way dad took us out after we visited that Rocky fellow?"

"Rocky fell… Oh, the Rockefeller Mausoleum." Leo stifled a laugh. "I remember going there, but I don't remember how we got out."

"I do," Gwen said. "Remember when you had to pee so bad you almost went on one of the tombstones? Dad took us to a building with bathrooms so they wouldn't ban our family from the cemetery."

"Oh yeah. The building made out of rocks."

"If you say so," Gwen humored her brother. "Follow me, but stay down and be quiet."

The three crept through the brush, around tombstones and onto another of the maze-like lanes that snaked through the cemetery. They heard cars whizzing by on a much busier road that lay just beyond some thick hedges.

"There's the exit gate leading onto Broadway," Gwen said, her chest puffed up with pride for remembering how to get out.

"That's what I was afraid of," Leo added, staring toward the exit road.

"What?" Gwen asked, following his gaze. Then she let out an uncharacteristic moan.

Hammy remained in the dark, in so many ways. "What are you guys talking about? Are we leaving this place or not?"

"Not." Leo looked from Hammy to Gwen. "Now what?"

Gwen saw the confusion on Hammy's face. "The gate is closed. I should have figured as much. It's long past the cemetery closing time. Nobody is supposed to be in here except the guards and those stupid lamplight tours."

As if on cue, a booming voice echoed from the direction of the bleak stone building that the trio had just walked around. "Hey!! What are you kids doing in here?"

Gwen didn't even bother trying to figure out who spoke. She just barked a single command. "Run!!!" She said as she turned and followed her own advice. Before any of them had time to think, they took off at a sprint back into the dusky heart of the cemetery.

CHAPTER SEVEN

Out of the Cemetery

The three of them ran along the asphalt road with Gwen in the lead. Every now and then she shouted random directions, and they changed course like a small and disorganized gaggle of geese.

Before Hammy collapsed from exhaustion, Gwen barked, "Into the trees."

Leo panted, Hammy wheezed, and Gwen looked as if she had been on a leisurely stroll through the park. Hammy considered mentioning something about the unfairness of it all, but his own heavy breathing prevented him from commenting.

Once Leo stopped panting, he said, "First, James and his goony friend send us into the cemetery. Then we're chased by a headless horseman and hunted down by the cemetery police. I realize Halloween is supposed to be creepy, but this is ridiculous."

Between heavy gasps, Hammy managed to reply, "I'm sorry about getting you guys into this mess. I feel like it's all my fault."

"It is all your fault, but we can discuss that later." Gwen was still lying on her stomach while she peered through the leafless branches of undergrowth. "For now, we have to figure out a way to the South Gate."

Leo pointed. "The South Gate is that way."

"Obviously dear brother." Gwen's voice sounded wicked enough to scare the local spirits. "In case you forgot, we've got cemetery guards and a headless horseman on our tail."

"Thanks for reminding me," Leo acknowledged.

"Lights," Hammy contributed.

"Care to elaborate?" Gwen suggested.

Hammy cast an irritated glance in Gwen's direction. "We can detect when the cemetery guards are nearby because of the headlights on their truck. And it's easy to spot the horseman guy because of his glowing head. So all we have to do is keep a lookout for either of those lights, and we'll be fine."

"You forgot one little thing." Gwen's voice revealed her annoyance with Hammy's plan.

"What one little thing?"

"What are we supposed to do when we see the lights?"

Leo answered for Hammy. "Hide, like we're doing now."

"And hope they don't spot us," Hammy added.

"Hope is good for school problems," Gwen said. "Like, I hope we have a substitute teacher in math class, or I hope we don't have a test in science class. I'd like a little better game plan for escaping this cemetery in one piece."

Leo had much more experience when it came to dealing with his sister's foul mood than Hammy. "Okay, how's this? We run as fast as we can until we're out of this place. If we notice any strange lights coming toward us, we split up and hide. They might catch one of us, but the other two could escape."

Neither Hammy nor Gwen appreciated Leo's idea, but they had no time to voice their opinions.

"This way," Leo whispered. He bolted out onto the asphalt road again and kept going without offering any opportunities for a counterproposal.

After calling Leo a few choice names unsuitable for such hallowed grounds, Gwen followed her brother onto the road. Upon a quick survey of his surroundings in a fog-enshrouded cemetery, Hammy decided to join his friends. He panicked at the sound of galloping hoofbeats, until he realized it was only his heart hammering in his chest.

After what seemed like the remainder of October and most of November, the trio reached the South Gate. Unlike the rest of the cemetery, the entrance was bathed in light from the nearby town and from the ancient-looking lamp posts standing sentinel over the visitor parking lot.The trio threw themselves at the gate, hoping it would be unlocked, but they were disappointed.

"Now what?" Leo scanned from Gwen to Hammy.

"Climb over?" Hammy suggested, looking at the endless row of tall, spiked bars surrounding the cemetery.

"Easy," Gwen said. "But what would you two do once I got over?"

Neither Hammy nor Leo were offended by Gwen's presumption. Leo pointed to the left-hand side of the gate, between two towering stone pillars. "We might be able to climb over that part."

The spiked poles of the cemetery fence were imposing, but the section to the left of the South Gate dipped much lower.

"I don't know," Hammy said. " I still don't understand how we're supposed to climb over."

Before Hammy's companions could resolve the dilemma, a booming voice echoed through the sacred grounds, coming from the direction of the Old Dutch Burial Grounds. "There they are."

Under the best of circumstances, a voice coming from the burial grounds would have been unsettling. On this unusual Halloween evening, it was particularly frightening. Hammy recognized the same security guard who had confronted them earlier. He strode toward the three trespassing youth with an unwelcoming glower on his face.

At the same time, Hammy spotted a group of tourists finishing their cemetery lamplight tour. The South Gate fence began swinging open in slow motion, to let the group out. The security guard also saw the gate opening and rushed to block their escape route.

"Now we don't have a choice," Leo shouted. "Get over here, Hammy."

Leo crouched down and put his hands out. "Let's help him over, sis." Gwen intertwined her fingers with Leo's so that they made a basket with their hands. "Put your foot in here, Hammy. We'll give you a hand."

"But—" Hammy stammered.

"I'll count to three," Gwen bellowed. "If you're not here by the time I'm done counting, we're going over without you. One—"

Hammy swung his right foot up into the makeshift stirrup offered by the twins. Before he could even grasp ahold of the iron bars on the fence, Gwen and Leo lifted him into the air.

Hammy started tipping toward one of the pointed fence spikes before gaining a foot hold on one of the horizontal rails that held the vertical poles together. Once his feet were planted on the rails, he grasped near the peak of the spear-like poles and clung to them with all his might. He was now crouched near the top of the fence, but he had no idea what to do next.

The twins scrambled up the iron barrier like children climbing a jungle gym. In a matter of seconds, they were both standing on the other side.

"Jump, Hammy!!" Gwen commanded, leaving little room for debate.

Hammy peered down at the distant ground, four feet away. He swayed back and forth, trying to muster the courage to leap.

Except mustering was never his strong suit, so he swayed a bit longer than Gwen could tolerate. "I don't know about you," she said to Leo, "but I'm not waiting around while Hammy sits on that fence like a chicken waiting for the fox." With that, she turned and began walking away from the cemetery and toward the Headless Horseman Bridge.

Hammy squeezed his eyes shut, took a deep breath and launched himself from the dizzying heights of the iron fence. He felt the wind rush past him as he hurtled to the unforgiving ground where he crash-landed onto all fours, tearing a hole in his pants and scratching the palms of his hands.

Leo had almost caught up with Gwen, but he stopped and waved Hammy onward. By this time, Gwen closed in on the bridge where two familiar and repulsive figures stood, laughing at the antics of Hammy and the twins.

Their laughing grew somewhat more subdued as they noticed the look on Gwen's face. Ely inched his way behind James and peered over his partner's shoulder. James hid behind Hammy's *Legend of Sleepy Hollow* book as if it could protect him from the wrath of Gwen.

Hammy nearly caught up with the twins when Gwen barked out four words. "Hand over the book."

James held the book out. "Okay, okay. No need to get all…"

James and Ely both stared over the top of Gwen toward the South Gate. Their eyes doubled in size, and they began walking backwards, still holding Hammy's book.

"What in the name of—" James' voice wavered with fear, and his face turned the same color as the marble statues in the cemetery.

At that moment, screams of terror flew through the air from the direction of the South Gate.

Gwen, about to reach for the book, turned her head to investigate what was causing all the commotion. She stopped dead in her tracks and exclaimed in a hoarse voice, "Not you again?"

Hammy and Leo stared in dread at the beast galloping full-speed through the stampeding crowd of screaming tourists. People were running in every direction, trying to escape the massive horse that strode through the cemetery gates. The rider scanned the crowd of people with its dark, triangular eyes, and then focused upon the bridge and its occupants.

James and Ely were frozen in place while Gwen, as usual, took charge. "Hammy and Leo… move it." Once again, the three were running away from a legend that had become a nightmare.

CHAPTER EIGHT

Legendary Swamp

For once, Hammy had little trouble keeping up with Gwen. His legs had a mind of their own, and that mind didn't like the thought of being apprehended by a headless creature astride a rampaging horse.

Gwen didn't bother consulting her companions about crossing the busy street. At the first minuscule gap in traffic, she darted across the road, oblivious to the blaring horns. Leo was right behind her.

Hammy, on the other hand, feared reckless drivers nearly as much as he feared creatures from the cemetery, so he looked both ways… at least three times. When it became clear that, safe crossing or not, Gwen had no intention of waiting for him, Hammy bolted across the street, to the shelter of a welcoming sidewalk on the other side.

Leo ran slower than his sister, in hopes that his cautious friend would catch up. He turned his head and yelled, "Hurry, Hammy! We have to keep up with Gwen, and she won't slow down for anybody or anything."

Hammy willed his legs to sprint faster and his lungs to stop hurting. He had run more in the past hour than he normally did in a month. If he ran this fast in gym class, the coach wouldn't always yell at him. The next fifteen minutes faded to a blur as the three fugitives splashed through one mud puddle after another on the sidewalks of Sleepy Hollow.

Approaching a familiar intersection, Hammy's energy dwindled. He glanced over his shoulder, expecting to catch sight of the horse and rider, but no boogey man reared its ugly, orange head. At least that's what Hammy thought. When he turned back around, he came face to pumpkin with another diabolical villain. This one also had a jack-o-lantern head but did not sit astride a black stallion. Instead, it stood in the middle of Beekman Street, its scarecrow body less than five yards from where Hammy stood, frozen with fear. He tried to scream, but nothing came out of his mouth. He just stared at yet another haunting creature.

Whereas the Headless Horseman rode a demon steed, this creature stood at motionless attention, sporting a demonic grin that covered an excessive portion of its face. Razor-sharp teeth lined the bottom and top of the creature's gaping mouth.

Beneath the massive head hung a scrawny body that consisted of twined pumpkin vines, tangled around one another and sticking out of canvas robes. A faded orange scarf dangled around its neck and swung down toward a hay bale that the scarecrow stood upon.

Hammy willed himself to run, but his legs refused to cooperate and his lungs burned from his dash down Broadway. He prepared for the creature to pounce and devour him in a single gulp when a hand settled upon his shoulder, and he nearly crumpled to the ground.

"What are you doing, Hammy?" Despite the impatience in Leo's voice, Hammy welcomed it with open ears. "Gwen is three blocks ahead of us, we've got a headless horseman on our tail, and you're standing here admiring the Halloween decorations."

"Decorations?" Hammy stammered. "I thought—"

"It doesn't matter what you thought. I have no idea what happened to our headless friend, but I'd rather not hang around here to find out."

Hammy aimed one last glimpse at the harmless scarecrow and spied a giant clock towering over its orange head. He had seen this Halloween adornment a hundred times over the past few years, but tonight, even the most familiar sights and sounds seemed like waking nightmares.

Leo didn't wait for Hammy's contemplations. He started running again, no longer tolerant of his friend's slow pace. "Gwen will be hiding in Patriots Park. We can stop once we catch up to her. But for now, you need to force yourself to run a little further, Hammy," Leo shouted over his shoulder.

Hammy struggled to keep up, but even as Sleepy Hollow High School materialized out of the fog on the other side of the street, he became overwhelmed by a morbid sense of dread.

For some reason, the words Patriot Park sent a chill down Hammy's spine. He had visited the place many times, yet something about it seemed different on this crazy night. Hammy's stomach began to ache, and each pounding heartbeat warned him of impending doom.

On his left, Hammy sighted the middle school where this entire mess had begun with a stolen book. After crossing College Avenue, Leo and Hammy arrived at the park. The knot in Hammy's stomach tightened. Leo stopped at a statue and, as Hammy approached him, he put a finger to his lips in a signal for silence.

Hammy peered around, searching for Gwen. Leo wore a grim scowl on his face that set Hammy to worrying again. A loud hissing noise erupted from near the statue's base, causing Hammy to screech in fear. Visions of slithering snakes crawled through his mind, stopping occasionally to squeeze the life out of his dwindling supply of courage.

"Where are you?" Leo asked.

Hammy still had snakes on his mind when he heard Gwen's hissing voice rise from the grounds of the park. "Down here, where you two should be."

Leo flattened onto his belly beside his sister, but Hammy remained standing, as if in a trance. "This isn't one of those books you're always reading, Hammy," Leo whispered. "Quit the drama and get down here."

Hammy crawled down beside his friends, his body following Leo's directions, but his mind still in a stupor.

"Maybe it can't find us," Leo said, his breath returning to his overburdened lungs. "Maybe it has forgotten all about us and is still back in the cemetery."

Hammy turned toward Leo. "It isn't back in the cemetery, and it hasn't forgotten about us."

The conviction in Hammy's voice was out of character. Gwen and Leo stared at him, awaiting an explanation.

"The closer we got to the park, the more worried I felt. I had no idea why, until Leo mentioned my books," Hammy said, a slight tremor in his speech. "This place hasn't always been called Patriots Park. In *The Legend of Sleepy Hollow*, it's called Wiley's Swamp."

While the expression on Leo's face said, *Huh?* Gwen's face revealed a less subtle message: *Explain yourself, immediately, or the Headless Horseman will have to protect you … from me.*

"This is where Ichabod Crane first spotted the Headless Horseman," Hammy continued. "I think this is where it wanted us to go all along."

"Sssssssshhhh!!" Gwen hissed. "Listen!!"

At first, Hammy and Leo heard nothing, but they were reluctant to admit it. When Gwen heard things, she preferred that others heard them too.

After a moment of silence, Leo detected the same sound as Gwen. The familiar clip-clop of horse's hooves filled the air. "That's got to be him."

"I don't remember seeing anyone else riding horses down the streets of Tarrytown." Gwen's tone matched the chilly temperature outside.

"Technically, we're still in Sleepy Hollow," Hammy contributed.

Leo and Gwen stared at their bespectacled companion with expressions that implied they might just decide to push him out into the street if he didn't stop getting technical sometime soon.

Hammy changed the subject before they decided to follow their evil glares with evil actions. "What do we do now?"

"It's too late to try and escape." Leo stopped talking as the hoofbeats grew louder by the moment. "If we try to run, we don't have a chance. Besides, I have no idea where we'd run from here. Hammy's house isn't very close, and ours is even further."

The hoofbeats grew louder. The horse neared the monument, then stopped. A heavy silence hung over Patriots Park until the clopping sound began again. It didn't continue down Broadway as it had before. Instead, it sounded as if it turned into the park, circling the statue where the three trembling sticks were hiding.

CHAPTER NINE

Ghouls on Parade

Steady hoofbeats continued around the statue while the three teens held their breath. Gwen glimpsed the horse's bobbing head as it rounded the base of the monument. She hugged the cold ground and signaled for the boys to remain silent.

The horse, rather than turning in their direction, continued toward the center of the park. Gwen started to crawl toward the front of the statue, signaling for Hammy and Leo to follow her. Once they got out to the sidewalk that ran between the road and the park, Gwen whispered, "We're going to have to make another run for it."

"Run where?" Leo's solemn face reflected the gravity of the situation.

Gwen turned to Hammy. "Didn't you say your mom is working at the Tarrytown Police Station tonight?"

Hammy thought for a moment. His brain was as foggy as the night. "She's working tonight. I don't know if she'll be at the station though."

"It doesn't matter if she's there or not. That's where we've got to head." Gwen started walking along the sidewalk, crouching down and looking toward the center of the park where they had last seen The Headless Horseman.

They crept along the walkway in stealth mode until Gwen started jogging. "I have no idea where our pumpkin-headed buddy is, but I have a feeling that he's not far behind us. We won't be safe until we're inside the police station."

Hammy wasn't sure if he had much running left in him, but he was positive he didn't want to be apprehended by a galloping ghost. So he mustered his waning strength and struggled to keep up with the twins. After a half mile, they had left Sleepy Hollow and turned onto Tarrytown's Main Street where a handful of people milled about, oblivious to the mounted demon that was roaming nearby.

"We missed the Halloween parade," Hammy moaned.

Leo cast an exasperated glare in Hammy's direction. Gwen voyaged one step further. "Oh, yeah. I forgot all about the parade. Gee, it's too bad we couldn't watch it. We must have had something else to do tonight. Oh, yeah. We were helping our friend get his stupid book back and then we got chased by an evil horseman from the eighteenth century."

Hammy tried his best to ignore Gwen's sarcasm. "I was hoping to see Mr. Holland."

"What are you talking about?" Gwen's tone maintained its frigid bite.

Hammy refused to look at Gwen for fear of being frozen by her chilly glare. "Remember in class today, Leo? Mr. Holland said he was going to be in the parade tonight. He said he would throw us some extra candy if he spotted us."

"No, I don't remember Hammy. I was too busy watching you try to find your missing book."

"Sorry I brought it up."

Gwen fired her final shot. "You should be. Now quit dawdling. If I hear that horse again, you're on your own. I'm not waiting for you any more."

They jogged down Main Street, Hammy taking the lead for once. He had lived in Tarrytown his entire life and could navigate its streets with his eyes closed. On this particular evening, he was tempted to do just that. He guided his friends past a gigantic music hall, a small gift shop and a medium sized restaurant. The drizzle of rain had driven most of the parade watchers away, leaving the sidewalks deserted.

"That's Washington Street ahead," Hammy said. "We're about halfway to the station."

Gwen's intolerance for Hammy's slow pace magnified her already cranky mood. "We'll never make it at this rate," she complained as she marched to the front of the pack. Halfway across Washington Street, Gwen screeched to an unannounced halt and wailed, "Ewwww!!" She stopped so abruptly that Leo collided into her.

Upon hearing Gwen's strange cry, Hammy crouched low and spun about. He scanned Main Street for an imminent attack from their headless stalker.

Gwen lifted her left foot, wrinkled her nose and muttered another, "Ewwwww!" The bottom of her shoe was covered in fresh, green, aromatic horse manure. Leo fought to keep from laughing and was losing the battle.

While Hammy clutched his chest as if his heart had exploded, Gwen tried scraping the bottom of her shoe on the sidewalk's edge. Then she whipped it off her foot and began banging it on the concrete. "I hate horse crap. I hate horses. I hate—"

Leo interrupted her. "I think we've got bigger problems than horse poop." He glanced up and down Main Street. "Where there's horse manure, there's bound to be horses. Why would horses be roaming the streets of Tarrytown if—"

No sooner had the words left his mouth, when a dreadful sound drowned out the patter of raindrops. The clip-clop of hooves grew louder by the second, except for this time, it sounded as if more than one horse was approaching.

The hoof beats grew louder as Gwen struggled to replace her shoe, poop and all.

"Hurry," Hammy whimpered. "It's getting closer."

"THEY are getting closer," Leo countered, as two horses and two riders appeared out of the dark mist, cantering up Washington Street.

Gwen hunched over, tying her shoelaces while glancing up at the mysterious figures approaching through the autumn haze.

"Forget your shoes. Just run," Leo shouted, already starting to shuffle sideways down Main Street as if half his body wanted to wait for Gwen while the other half tried to make a dash for safety.

A voice rang out from one of the horse riders. "Who hates horses?" It sounded nothing like the voice of a headless horseman. "Is that Hammy and the twins?"

Leo recognized the two fully-headed horsemen and called out, "Randy and Shelly? What are you guys doing riding horses… in the middle of Tarry town… at this time of night?"

Randy Purcell smiled and waved to his classmate. "Hey Leo. How come you weren't at soccer practice after school today?" Before he gave Leo a chance to answer, he continued. "We were in the parade tonight, with the Tarrytown Equestrians."

Tammy took over where her brother left off. "We were supposed to give Mr. Holland a ride home, but—"

Gwen didn't bother listening to the rest. Unlike everyone else at

Sleepy Hollow Middle School, she wasn't a huge Tammy Purcell fan. Nobody was as big a fan of Tammy Purcell as Tammy Purcell. Gwen couldn't help glancing over at the bus stop bench on the nearby sidewalk where a beaming photo of Wanda Purcell adorned the back of the bench above the words, "Hudson Valley's #1 Realtor." Wanda had the exact same curly blonde hair and steely gray eyes as both of her children who were the only other set of twins in sixth grade at Sleepy Hollow Middle School.

Tammy transferred the reins of her horse to her left hand and twirled her golden locks with her right. "What are you guys doing here?" She pointed the question at Gwen who pretended not to hear.

Hammy attempted to fill the awkward silence. "We were at the Sleepy Hollow Cemetery when this huge—"

Leo interrupted. "What Hammy is trying to say is that we were watching the parade and now we're headed home. Right Hammy?"

"Uhhhh…"

"Yep. Just headed home," Gwen reiterated and started walking back down Main Street. "So peachy to see you two. We'll catch you at school on Monday."

"What did you tell them that for?" Hammy muttered to Leo.

"Oh, I don't know. Maybe I'm not too anxious for the Purcell twins to tell everyone that we've been hanging out at the cemetery and communing with imaginary demons on horses."

"But it's not imaginary."

Gwen sided with her brother for a change. "You know it's not imaginary. I know it's not imaginary. But I'm not sure our friends would believe we spent the weekend with a decapitated horseman." Gwen's strides grew longer. "Speaking of our galloping ghoul, let's pick up the pace before he shows up again."

Gwen began jogging, and the other two followed in her tracks, eyes scanning to and fro in search of unwelcome pursuers.

Soon, they spotted the back of the police station. Main Street curved to the right, wrapping around the public buildings and ended at Depot Plaza where the three of them cut through an abandoned parking lot. The police station, with its gleaming white tower sticking out of the roof, stood a short way beyond the parking lot. Hammy breathed a sigh of relief.

His sigh or relief was drowned by Leo's moan of dread. For standing a dozen yards in front of them, blocking their entrance to the police station, was the midnight black stallion, steam rising from its flanks and bizarre rider still on its back.

"It looks like we're going to have to go with Plan B," Leo said to his two companions.

"I hope it's better than Plan A," Gwen replied

"What's Plan B?" Hammy asked.

Leo and Gwen looked at each other and shouted, "Run!!!"

CHAPTER TEN

Unexpected Train Ride

Gwen took the lead as they ran out of the parking lot and came to a nearly deserted road. Before she sprinted too far ahead, Hammy yelled, "We're going to be trapped if we go this way."

"Do you have any better suggestions?" Gwen yelled back, not bothering to slow down.

They began to cross the multi-lane road, but as soon as they got to the middle, they ran into a barrier. A black, wrought-iron fence served as a divider between the north and south-bound traffic lanes.

"Now what?" Leo asked, as he came to an abrupt halt. Before anyone answered his question, a loud whinnying sound filled the air, and the Headless Horseman exited the parking lot, clacking its way onto the street, headed directly toward them.

"You can stay here and play with our creepy friend," Gwen said, between heavy breaths. "I'm going over the fence." With that, she placed both of her hands on top of the sturdy barrier and rolled first one leg over, then the other. A narrow strip of grass broke her sidelong fall onto the ground with the asphalt road only inches away.

Leo followed his sister, making the hurdle look easy. As soon as he got over, he shouted back to Hammy, "That was a cinch. C'mon Hamm—" But his friend had disappeared.

Leo and Gwen stared in disbelief as Hammy dashed up the road toward a break in the fence and a crosswalk on the street. The twins shook their heads. Leo's shake was one of amazement, and Gwen's was one of disgust. After they had finished their head-shaking, the twins crossed the final two lanes to find Hammy loping down the sidewalk, putting most of his effort into avoiding eye contact.

Halfway across the street, the Headless Horseman had stopped at the barrier. Leo smiled and winked at Hammy. "It appears you're not the only one who can't make it over the fence."

"Are you crazy?" Gwen had a unique way of asking a question and answering it, all in one blunt statement. "Nothing has stopped that creep so far. What makes you think a little fence is going to get in his way? We need to find our way out of here and fast."

As Gwen spoke, the horse and rider crossed back over the street, away from where they were standing.

Hammy bravely ignored Gwen and grinned at Leo. "You were right. It can't get over." He pointed toward their retreating nemesis.

"I wouldn't be so sure," Gwen replied, beginning to shuffle down the street.

Rather than taking the Hammy route around the fence, the Headless Horseman galloped directly at the black, metal barricade. Once it was only a few feet away, it raised its front hooves and flew into the air, like a demon reindeer on Christmas, easily clearing the fence and hurtling right at Hammy and Leo.

Gwen, who was halfway down the street, hollered back at the two boys, "The train depot is straight ahead. Don't slow down until you're there."

Sure enough, less than fifty yards in front of them was the brown and red-rocked Tarrytown railroad station.

With the click-clack of horse's hooves beating in their ears, Hammy and Leo sprinted toward Gwen and the solid old building. They realized that, if they stayed to the right-hand side of the depot between the station and the railroad fencing, the horse and rider couldn't follow them. The passage was too narrow for such a large animal to navigate.

Sure enough, the maddening sounds of horseshoes on asphalt disappeared once the three artless dodgers made their way to the other side of the depot. Hammy recognized one inviting sign hanging on the wall of the building. "I wish the bakery was open. A donut would be good right now."

For the third time that evening, the twins directed a look of disgust at Hammy. Gwen spoke for both of them. "If you mention food one more time, you can finish this little adventure on your own."

Before Hammy had a chance to defend himself, Gwen continued in the same indignant tone. "We're not safe yet. As long as we're anywhere near that bozo and his horse, we can't stop and rest..." She glared at Hammy. "…or eat."

We've got to find someplace where the horse can't follow us." Gwen scanned the nearby buildings, but they were all closed for the evening. "Where can we go that's—"

Leo had the answer before Gwen finished her question. "Stairs!!!" He shouted.

Gwen scowled. "What are you talking about?"

"Over there," Leo pointed down the sidewalk where, sure enough, a set of stairs rose toward a pedestrian platform that crossed over the railroad tracks. "There's no way that beast can climb up those steps."

All three tore across the platform toward the stairs, but halfway to their destination, the horseman loped into view, heading in the same direction as Hammy and the twins. The only chance they had was to reach the pedestrian walkway before their pursuer; but it was a slim chance given the speed of the stallion.

Gwen had just arrived at the bottom of the stairway when she turned and spotted the huge beast looming over Hammy like a wolf over a rabbit.

"Keep going," Gwen commanded her brother, and she ran back in the direction of the Headless Horseman. She had the element of surprise on her side since the orange-headed demon was focused on Hammy. She grabbed the horse's reins and gave them a forceful tug. The horse rocked back on its haunches and reared upward, its hooves pawing the air, only inches from Gwen's head.

"Run, Hammy!!" Gwen cried.

Hammy hesitated before shooting off toward the stairs. Gwen, darting in front of the confused horse and rider, followed Hammy to the steps. They both dashed up them, as fast as their legs would go. They reached the top at the same time and continued sprinting on the platform above the railroad tracks where they saw a north-bound train pulling into the station.

As soon as they reached the end of the walkway, they scurried down the steps and onto another platform, on the other side of the tracks. They observed people milling about on the arriving train, some preparing to disembark in Tarrytown and others headed further north. But, because of the passenger train blocking their view, they couldn't spot the horse or its cargo on the other side of the tracks.

When the north-bound train finally departed the station, the mounted nightmare stared directly at them, from across the tracks. Although he was temporarily unable to reach them from the other side of the station, they knew that he would eventually find a way to cross and, when he did, they were trapped.

The platform on which they stood was surrounded by an insurmountable fence with no easy route of escape. The sunken railroad tracks were directly in front of them. Behind them was a high fence and the the Hudson River. The platforms to their right and left were both dead ends.

"Now what?" Leo asked, a hint of panic in his voice.

They all fretted in silence, no one offering an answer. At that moment, a new train arrived, this one south-bound and gliding on the rails closest to their platform. Once again, their view of the horseman was blocked, and they glanced helplessly at each other.

Somehow the beast seemed even more scary when it was out of view. With or without his steed, the horseman was liable to sneak up on them at any moment and take them by surprise. They felt trapped and helpless.

The twins were nearly caught off guard when Hammy shouted. "Quick. The train only stops for a minute. Jump on."

Hammy didn't wait for the others. He walked to one of the open train doors, hopped up two steps and was on board. An announcement blared over the platform speakers. "All aboard. The train will be departing in one minute."

Gwen and Leo followed Hammy, but with cautious hesitation, still unsure of why they were climbing onto to a train.

Hammy kept moving once he was in the gleaming metal car. He opened the sliding door that revealed a passenger section that contained very few passengers and lots of empty seats. Gwen caught up to him and smacked her hand down on his shoulder. "Are you crazy? What are we doing?"

Hammy ignored her and made for the first empty seat on the opposite side of the train. Instead of sitting in the spacious bench seat, he kneeled onto it and gazed out toward the Tarrytown depot.

Gwen's voice was apprehensive. "We have to get off this train before it leaves. What are we going to—"

Hammy pointed toward the boarding platform outside. Overhead lights struggled through hazy fog to light the depot. "You can get off if you want," Hammy said. "Say hello to our headless friend while you're out there."

The horseman sat astride his black steed and peered through the train windows at the three of them. The train rolled out of the station.

Hammy plopped down with an uncomfortable slump, his shoulders trembling from fear and exhaustion.

The seat was wide enough for all three of them, and they perched in silence for a few seconds, the clickety-clack of the train growing faster and sounding more and more like the hoofbeats of their pursuer. Finally Gwen spoke. "What do we do now? Where does this train go? How do we pay for our tickets?"

Hammy had a plan. He had no idea if it was a good one, but it was a plan. "We ride the train and get off at the next stop in Irvington. That will only take a couple of minutes and the conductor probably won't make it to our car by then. Once we're in Irvington, we can ride the next train back to Tarrytown. By that time, the creep on the horse will be gone."

Both Leo and Gwen stared at Hammy for a moment before smiling. "That's genius!" Leo said, as he slumped back in the seat, looking every bit as exhausted as his companions.

"Don't make yourself too comfortable. We'll be in Irvington in a couple minutes. The train only stops for a few seconds, so we'll have to get off right away." Hammy stood and made his way toward the nearest exit. He had ridden the train many times before, so he knew his plan could work.

The train neared Irvington but didn't seem to be shedding any speed. Hammy's confidence began to wane. He didn't want to say anything to his companions, but he sensed something was wrong. In a flash, the Irvington station zipped by their windows. They hadn't even slowed down.

Leo was looking out one of the broad train windows. "Hey. The sign at that last station said *Irvington*. Why aren't we stopping?"

The twins turned to face Hammy who appeared as if he might be sick at any moment. He stared back at them and muttered, "This must be an express train."

"A what?" Leo and Gwen said at the same time.

"An express train," Hammy repeated, afraid to say more.

"What does that mean?" Gwen demanded.

Hammy slouched back to where they had been sitting before. He plopped down onto the seat with a look of anguish on his face. "It means we're going all the way to New York City."

CHAPTER ELEVEN

Escape to the City

"All the way to New York City?" Leo's jaw dropped.

"We can't go all the way to New York City," Gwen said, as if daring Hammy to disagree.

"Really?" Hammy's voice became shrill. "How about if you head up to the front and tell the engineer that? I bet he'll turn this train around and take us straight home."

"You don't seem to understand," Gwen ignored Hammy's outburst. "It's not as if this is some minor inconvenience. Do I need to start listing the problems with this little train ride? Let's see... we don't have tickets, we don't have our phones, we have no idea what to do once we're in the city—"

"It's not like I planned this," Hammy countered. "Do you think I wanted to go to New York City on Halloween?"

Leo jumped into the fray. "It's nobody's fault, so cool your jets, both of you." He turned to Gwen. "Our only other choice was to stay in Tarrytown and deal with the headless dude. Is that what you wanted to do?"

Before his sister had a chance to answer, Leo turned to Hammy. "Are you sure this train doesn't stop until we're in the city?"

Hammy tore his eyes off Gwen and focused on Leo. "It's not rocket science. The regular train stops in Irvington, and the express train doesn't. If this was the regular train we'd have made at least two stops by now." Another train station whizzed by outside the window, as if to prove Hammy's point.

"You've been on the train a lot more than we have. What do we do next?"

Hammy plopped back down into one of the long, bench seats. "It's not the end of the world. We can still ride the train back to Tarrytown. It'll just take longer."

"What about tickets?" Gwen asked, forcing her voice to sound conversational rather than accusatory.

"That is a problem," Hammy answered, his eyes wandering everywhere except Gwen's face.

As if to prove Hammy's point, an announcement blared over the train's speakers. "Have your tickets ready when the conductor arrives at your car."

"Oh, oh." Leo pointed to the opposite end of the rail car. "Here she comes."

Gwen looked where her brother pointed and said, "I need to go to the bathroom, and I think you two should join me."

Hammy screwed up his face. "That's gross. Why would we need to join you in the bathroom?"

Leo opened the bathroom door, and Gwen pulled Hammy inside. Leo joined them and shut the door, sliding the status bar to *occupied*.

"Why are we in here?" Hammy peered around the limited confines of the bathroom in disgust. "We've barely got enough room for one person, and it stinks." He plugged his nose with a thumb and index finger.

"If you want to pay for our tickets, be my guest." Gwen swept her hand in the direction of the bathroom door. "Otherwise, keep your voice down."

The three focused on not touching anything nor, for that matter, even breathing the foul air. Hammy continued to pinch his fingers over his nose, trying hard not to gag.

"What if I have to..." Leo paused and avoided eye contact with his sister. "Really use the bathroom?"

Before Gwen had the time to form her hand into a proper fist, Leo added, "Only kidding."

After a brief silence that stretched to infinity, Gwen whispered to the two boys, "Which of you is going to stick your head out the door to check if the ticket lady is gone?"

"Why does it have to be one of us?" Leo asked.

"First of all, because if I stick my head out, and she sees me, our ticket collecting friend might come in here and drag me out. There's slightly less of a chance she'll do that with you guys," Gwen explained

with more than a hint of impatience in her voice. "And next, I said so."
The impatient tone was matched by an impatient glare.

"How about we use *rock, paper, scissors* to decide," Hammy
suggested to Leo.

"Or you could do it, since this whole mess is your fault."

Hammy couldn't argue with Leo's logic nor did he enjoy arguing
with anyone's logic. He pushed down on the silver door handle,
causing the little slider to change from *occupied* to *vacant*. He poked his
head a couple inches outside the door and received an angry glare
from a lady waiting for an open restroom. He tried his best to ignore
the glare and swiveled his head from right to left so he had a view of
the entire railroad car.

"The coast is clear," Hammy reported.

"We're not on the coast," Gwen informed him as she barreled over
Hammy in her rush to exit the aromatic little cubicle.

All three of them piled out of the bathroom and were greeted by the
agitated stares of other passengers. "If I remember right, this train only
makes two stops. We stay on until the second one," Hammy said.

"Then where will we be?" Gwen interrogated Hammy.

Hammy peered at Gwen as if she was an annoying little kid. "New
York City?" He was quite certain they had covered all of this before.

"Duh," Gwen scowled. "But where in New York City?"

Hammy pondered for a moment. *What was the name of that place?*
"Oh, yeah. Grand Central Station."

"Isn't that slightly massive?" Leo asked.

"With a lot of people?" Gwen added.

Hammy's irritation was starting to show. "Well, it isn't Sleepy
Hollow. But it doesn't matter. We won't be staying long. As soon as we
get there, we'll catch the next train back to Tarrytown."

The view outside the train window seemed almost as if they had
traveled to another world. Enormous brick buildings and busy streets
replaced the tranquil waters of the Hudson River and the peaceful
hamlets they had been traveling through. The train intercom system
blared out something about Harlem, and Hammy reminded his friends
to stay on the train until the next stop.

Within moments, the streets and buildings disappeared and the
world went dark, as the train submerged into the underground world
of the city. Hammy had ridden the same route many times with his
family. But the experience was a novelty to the Skyler twins, and their
eyes expanded with each new change of scenery.

Soon, the intercom crackled, "Next stop, Grand Central Station. This is our final destination. Be sure to disembark here and take all of your belongings with you."

Gwen muttered something about wishing they had a few more belongings to take with them while Hammy led them to the sliding doors of their train car. Soon, they were standing on a busy platform watching the train disgorge its teeming passengers, most of whom did not even slow down as they detrained and made their way toward the hubbub of the main station.

"Now what?" Gwen asked, for the second time that night.

"Back to Tarrytown." Hammy flashed his old familiar grin.

Gwen didn't find Hammy's smile contagious. "I already knew that. But how… when… where?"

"Calm down, little sister." Leo ignored Gwen's glare. "We can't expect Hammy to think of everything."

After a moment's pause, Leo continued. "But I hope you know what we do next, Ham."

"Well, I think we—"

"You think?" Gwen bellowed. "We're lost in the middle of New York City, and you think?"

"We're not lost," Hammy muttered. "Excuse me if I've never gotten off the train and then gotten right back on again. That's not the normal way it works."

"I figured that we would stay on the same train, and end up riding back the same way we came," Leo said. "How about if we ask one of the train conductors?"

As soon as Leo finished speaking, another train pulled into the station on the other side of the platform. The commuters from the original Tarrytown express had disbursed when the people from the new train began streaming out like bees flying from their hive.

Hammy searched for anyone in uniform who might be able to help them. After a moment, he spotted a uniformed employee in the far back of the new train. He began scurrying in that direction, then stopped dead in his tracks. He stared in horror. Without turning back toward his friends, he stammered, "I've got some bad news, guys."

Gwen caught up to Hammy and tugged on his shoulder. "What are you talking about? I believe we've had more than our share of bad news for the day."

"Well, it just got worse," Hammy said, as he pointed in the direction of a unique passenger who had stepped off the train and was gazing about the cavernous train hall.

Gwen could only stare in the direction Hammy was pointing while her brother joined them. The zombie-like expression on Leo's face foreshadowed his next words. "This is not good."

The Headless Horseman had ditched his trusty black steed. but seemed every bit as daunting without it. He scanned the thinning crowd, looking for someone or, in this case, three someones.

Gwen was the first to take action. "I have no idea where I'm going, but good luck keeping up with me." She hurtled toward the tunnel-like exit from the boarding area faster than she had run all day.

The last vision Hammy saw before turning to follow the twins, was the evil glare of his worst nightmare.

CHAPTER TWELVE

Debacle on Fifth Avenue

Now, more than ever, Hammy realized he had to keep up with the twins. Even with a glaring panel of white lights shining down from overhead, it seemed as if they were running into a dark tunnel. Hammy remembered, from previous trips to Grand Central Station, what happened at the end of the tunnel. It spilled out into a series of maze-like hallways that ran in all directions. If the three of them got separated, they would never find each other.

Hammy dashed to catch Leo, who sprinted close behind Gwen, and the three of them made their way down the corridors of Grand Central Station. Soon, they entered a massive, glistening concourse where thousands of people milled about. Gwen stopped in her tracks and gawked.

"Is it always this busy?" Leo wondered aloud.

"It's way busier earlier in the day," Hammy replied, looking back over his shoulder. "But we've got to keep going before you-know-who shows up."

"You can say his name," Gwen snapped. "It's not like he's Voldemort."

"The less I say it, the better," Hammy shot back.

As if thinking with one mind, the three began jogging through the expansive concourse. None of the many folks weaving about the place paid any attention to the young wanderers.

"Which way, Hammy?" Gwen demanded.

Hammy was clueless, but he had no intention of revealing that to Gwen. Under ordinary circumstances, he would suggest they stop at the information booth in the middle of the palatial room. However, he decided these circumstances weren't quite normal. "To those doors," he said, pointing to a series of arched passages straight ahead.

"Do you have any idea what you're doing?" Gwen asked, as they ran toward the exits.

Hammy wished Gwen would stop expecting him to know where he was going, because he usually didn't when he was in the city. But he started getting much better at making up answers on the spot. "To my sister's apartment," he replied.

"Your sisters—?" Gwen's question fell short of Hammy's rapidly retreating backside.

The next doors they found led to the outside and had a sign pointing to East 42nd Street. Immediately upon stepping outside, Leo ground to a halt and looked up. "Listen," he said, with his index finger covering his lips.

Hammy and Gwen glanced at each other with puzzled expressions on their faces.

Leo's eyes sparkled with wonder. He pointed to the cars slowly driving by in front of them. "There's a road down here..." He paused and pointed upward. "And there's another road over our heads."

Gwen continued staring at her brother with a look that asked, *and what is your point?*

Before the twins could start squabbling, Hammy spoke up. "I remember this street from the last time I was here." He hoped to change the subject before Gwen had a chance to ask him which way to go. "We turn right and follow this street." He pointed in the direction of a large bus rumbling slowly down the road.

They stepped out into the darkness, and rain fell in slow motion onto the street. Lights from cars, store windows and street lamps provided some illumination, but it still felt dreary and cold as the twins followed Hammy along the sparsely populated sidewalk.

"The last time I visited here, this street was crawling with people." Hammy hoped if he kept talking, Gwen would have less chance to bug him with questions he couldn't answer.

"That's interesting," Gwen said without meaning it. "Is there the slightest chance you know where you're going?"

"I already told you. We're going to my sister's apartment."

"I don't suppose you have any useful information about her apartment, such as the address or the general location?"

"Well..." Hammy stalled.

Gwen's scowl signaled that she wasn't thrilled with Hammy's answer… nor his stalling.

"I remember that the address had a bunch of fives in it."

Gwen's scowl continued to occupy most of her face.

"In fact, it seemed to be all fives." Hammy hoped his answer would relieve Gwen of the nasty scowl that seemed to spend way too much time on the front of her head.

Leo was relieved that someone else was on the receiving end of Gwen's hostile glares, but he felt an urgent desire to resume their escape from Grand Central Station and their stalking companion. Without a word, he started walking down the sidewalk. He had no idea where he was going until he got to a busy street. He looked up at the street sign as his friends caught up to him. "We're on the right track."

"How do you know where Hammy's sister lives?" Gwen challenged.

Leo's grin rotated toward Hammy. "You said your sister's address has a bunch of fives in it, right?" Leo obviously knew the answer to his own question.

"That's what I remember." Hammy's voice lacked conviction.

"This street is Fifth Avenue." Leo pointed to a blue street sign with white lettering.

"Then this must be the place," Gwen said with a smile that would force a grizzly bear back into hibernation.

"No this isn't it." Leo gave as good as he got. "But this might at least be the right street. Do you have any better ideas?"

When Gwen failed to answer, Hammy decided to go along with Leo's wild guess. "Yeah. This is the street. We turn this way." He pointed to the right, trying his best to look confident for Gwen's sake.

Leo didn't wait for any further discussion and began striding up Fifth Avenue. He hoped Hammy would figure out some kind of a destination, even if it was the wrong one. Besides, he didn't want a Headless Horseman catching up with them anytime soon, with or without a horse.

Every once in a while, the trio spied mingling groups of werewolves, vampires and other creatures of the night. All of them seemed to be enjoying Halloween in the city every bit as much as the trick-or-treaters back home in Sleepy Hollow and Tarrytown. Except the older revelers didn't appear to be looking for candy.

Each time Hammy crossed a street, he felt like he had embarked upon a new adventure. "The cars aren't so bad, but I swear the bike riders are out to get me," he grumbled to Leo.

As if navigating the city streets didn't provide enough excitement, all three of them kept looking back to check if they were being followed. They expected, at any minute, the Headless Horseman would swoop down on them and do whatever it was Headless Horsemen did.

At every intersection, while they stopped to scan each direction, about a dozen times, Gwen asked the same question. "Does this look familiar?"

And every time, Hammy said, "Not really." After about the fourth time, he tired of the question. After the dozenth time, he grew uncharacteristically cranky. "Why do you keep asking me the same question? Obviously, we aren't there yet. I have no idea where we are. When we arrive, you'll be the first one I—"

"We're there," Leo announced, happy to interrupt Hammy's tirade and to stop Gwen from repeating the same question over and over.

"We're where?" Gwen and Hammy asked at the same time.

"How do you know we're there?" Gwen asked. "You don't even know where *there* is. You've never been to Hammy's sister's apartment."

Leo ignored Gwen and stepped closer to Hammy. "Does this place look familiar to you, Ham?"

"Kind of. I mean, I think I've been here before, but—"

"This is a place with lots of fives, like you said." Leo pointed to the street signs once again. "555 Fifth Avenue qualifies as a place with a lot of fives in the address."

Hammy smiled. "I'm nearly positive this is the right place. Now I remember the time my dad and I visited my sister and..." He paused and surveyed the area. "Oh, oh."

Gwen erupted. "Tell me you did not just say oh, oh. I am not in the mood for oh, ohs."

Hammy now surveyed the ground instead of the buildings. "Do you guys see any apartments around here?"

Leo jumped in before Gwen had a chance to attack. "Are you sure your sister lives here, Hammy?"

Hammy avoided Gwen's glare. "No. I'm not sure at all. In fact, I'm sure she doesn't live here." He stepped behind Leo so Gwen would have a tougher time getting to him. "Now I remember this is where my sister worked, not where she lived."

Leo wasn't so sure he wanted to stand between Hammy and Gwen. It seemed less safe than standing out in the middle of Fifth Avenue. "And I don't suppose she would be working now, would she?"

Hammy glanced around at all the dark storefronts before answering. "I don't think she works at night."

Gwen remained surprisingly calm as she began to stride toward Hammy. "I think I know how the Headless Horseman became headless," she said through gritted teeth. "I bet he took his friends into New York City and got them lost." Her eyes glowed like two blazing coals, and her voice rose to one decibel below a scream. "And then one of his friends got tired of running around in the freezing rain and knocked his head off."

Leo took his life into his hands and remained between Gwen and Hammy. "Okay, settle down Gwen. Hammy is not the enemy here. We've got to remain calm and figure out what to do." He paused for a moment, then added, "Although *The Legend of Headless Hammy* would make a great name for a book."

Neither Gwen nor Hammy appreciated Leo's humor, but they appreciated each other even less at the moment.

Hammy tried to redeem himself. "I remember my sister's apartment wasn't far from where she worked. In fact," he said, "I think it's in that direction." He pointed up the same street they'd been walking on.

"You think it's in that direction?" Gwen asked. "That's wonderful. Maybe we can start walking that way and asking everyone if they've seen Hammy's sister. I bet they'll all be real helpful, and we'll find her in no time."

"Her name is Winnie."

"What?"

"Her name is Winnie, not Hammy's sister." Hammy no longer wanted to argue with Gwen. He never wanted to argue with Gwen, and this particularly dreadful evening was no exception.

"Okay fine, then." Gwen huffed. "We'll ask everyone if they've seen Winnie."

Leo interrupted. He squinted down the street in the direction from which they had just come. "We won't be asking anyone anything."

Gwen let out a breath of exasperation. "Of course we won't. I was only making the point..."

"Run!" Leo shouted. And he turned around and sprinted.

Hammy stood paralyzed, frozen in place. He didn't have to ask what had scared Leo, because he already knew.   When he looked down the street, his darkest fears were realized. Lumbering up Fifth Avenue, inconspicuous among the other costumed Halloween revelers was the horseless horseman, its orange head glowing, and its black cape flowing in the New York wind.

CHAPTER THIRTEEN

A Stroll in the Park

Leo raced back and grabbed Hammy by the arm. "Which part of RUN don't you understand?"

It made perfect sense. When being chased by a demonic beast, the best option was to run away. Yet Hammy couldn't seem to make his legs work. His eyes worked fine as they focused on the approaching monster. His ears couldn't help but detect Leo pleading with him to flee. But his legs would not cooperate, despite the imminent danger that lurched closer by the moment.

Leo tried to convince Hammy that it was a good idea to start running sooner rather than later. But Hammy remained frozen in place. Gwen pleaded with Hammy also, except her pleas sounded much more like commands.

"Come on, Hammy. Quit being ridiculous. You've got to run." When her cajoling had no effect, Gwen tried appealing to Hammy's sense of decency. "If you stay here, Leo will stay too, and you'll both be at the mercy of the brainless horseman. Do you really want that to happen?"

This snapped Hammy out of his reverie. His legs gained a little more strength, and he ran alongside the twins, but not fast enough. One glance back revealed that his ghoul friend was gaining ground and had almost caught up. "We're not going to be able to outrun him," Hammy groaned.

"I don't have to outrun him," Gwen replied. "I just have to outrun you. He can only catch one of us at a time."

This motivated Hammy to pick up his pace. He dashed through

columns of steam as they rose above the manhole covers. He wrinkled his nose and gagged. "What is that putrid smell?"

Gwen didn't bother turning around. "That's the scent of pure evil, and it will be the last thing you inhale if you don't hurry," she said, not slowing a bit.

After one more block, they saw what appeared to be a forest in the middle of the city. Leo pointed toward it. "Let's hide in those trees."

Hammy remembered the area from many of their family trips. "That's Central Park."

"I don't care if it's the Amazon rain forest," Gwen said. "That's where we're going."

They crossed the street, receiving a chorus of honks from irate drivers. After running a couple blocks, Leo veered to the right. Hammy tried his best to keep up, but after only a few seconds, he lost track of his friends.

"Pssst," Leo hissed at Hammy from the cover of surrounding trees and bushes a few feet off the busy street. "Down here."

Hammy crouched to join the twins in their hiding spot. "We should be safe here for a few minutes, but we can't stay here all night." He shivered as he spoke. "It's getting cold outside. I don't know about you guys, but I'm sopping wet from head to toe."

Leo nodded in agreement. "Let's hang here for a couple minutes and then try to find some place a little less soggy."

After a few moments passed, Gwen was eager to lead the way. "Stay close to the trees in case the headless guy shows up."

"Too late," Hammy yelped, jumping backward and practically knocking Gwen over. "He's already here."

"Watch where you're going," Gwen barked. She followed Hammy's gaze, then let out an involuntary screech.

Hammy was staring up at a huge figure on a massive horse that had risen onto its two hind legs. It wore a crazed expression with eyes bulging and front hooves flailing in the air. The rider was pointing right at the three kids as they huddled together, shivering in the night.

Gwen quickly recovered from her initial shock, then smacked Hammy on the top of his soggy head. "You idiot. It's only a stupid statue."

"How was I supposed to know?" Hammy rubbed the top of his head.

Before Gwen had the opportunity to inform Hammy that real horses weren't made of bronze and didn't stand motionless on a square pedestal, Leo interrupted. "But those horses are real." He pointed toward the interior of the park.

Hammy whirled around with an abrupt yelp. His outburst turned to an embarrassed sigh of relief once he realized that the horses he spied were attached to white and gold carriages. He was equally relieved to notice that the carriage drivers had their full compliment of body parts, including heads that did not resemble jack-o-lanterns in any way.

Leo pretended as if he hadn't heard Hammy's shrill outburst. "Those must be carriages for tourists to explore Central Park."

Hammy recovered his wits, if not his dignity. "We rode on those once. And remember, Mr. Holland said he drove Central Park carriages during the summer."

"No, I don't remember," Gwen added, "because I don't pay attention to every word Mr. Holland says. Sometimes he's kind of boring, if you ask me."

"I was just saying—"

Leo interrupted again. "We can discuss the merits of Mr. Holland's stories some other time. For now, we need to find someone who can help us. Let's go talk to one of those carriage drivers."

Hammy was reluctant to step out into the brightly lit open space. "What if the Headless Horseman sees us?"

"I doubt he would do anything with all these people around." Leo didn't wait for Hammy's reply. He walked toward the carriages, hoping to find a helpful tour guide. He approached the nearest one and, before he could say anything, a man in a gigantic top-hat smiled and asked, "How about a ride around the park? We'll be closing soon, so you can be my last tour of the evening."

"We don't have any money, but I was wondering—" Leo started.

As soon as the carriage driver heard the phrase, *don't have any money*, his smile disappeared, and he walked away from the three stranded teens. "You kids run along home. It must be past your bed time," he grunted over his shoulder.

Leo and Hammy restrained Gwen, whose eyes shot daggers at the rude fellow.

"Maybe he's having a bad day," Hammy surmised, hoping Gwen wouldn't turn her lethal glare on him.

Leo approached another of the carriage drivers. This one wore a cowboy hat with a billowing feather sticking out of one side. The man took one look at the three teens approaching him and held up his hand with his palm facing outward. "Sorry ladies and gentlemen," he signaled. "I just finished my last ride. It's time to put the horses to bed. But I'll be happy to give you a ride tomorrow."

Leo nodded toward Hammy. "Thanks, but my friend here has a question for you."

Hammy cast Leo a puzzled glare. "I do?"

"Yes. You were wondering about your favorite teacher."

"Oh that," Hammy stalled, trying to figure out what Leo was talking about. "Um… my teacher works in Central Park during the summer giving horse carriage rides. We… I mean I was wondering if you knew him."

The carriage driver smiled. "A lot of people work here during the summer. I'll need a little more information."

Gwen jumped into the conversation. "His name is Mr. Holland. He tells boring stories and he—"

Before Gwen finished her sentence, they all heard a phantom voice penetrating the misty silence. "Stop those kids."

They turned to see who had spoken and found themselves staring directly at the horrible visage of the Headless Horseman. Worse still, the black-cowled demon ran at full speed, in their direction.

"Quick, this way!" Gwen shouted as she turned and ran down a broad asphalt path that led deeper into the park.

The further they ran away from the carriages, the darker it got. Between rattling gasps, Hammy shouted, "Where is everyone?"

Gwen had also noticed how eerily deserted the park was, but she knew why. "We're the only ones stupid enough to be running through a dark forest, in the middle of New York City, on Halloween night."

Hammy glanced over his shoulder and realized their headless adversary was no longer pursuing them.

"I think we lost him," Leo called out to the other two.

The words had barely escaped his lips when the sound of galloping hoofbeats filled the air and shattered their hopes. Once again, Hammy's head swiveled around, hoping to see nothing but an empty park. His hopes were dashed to pieces. Bearing down on them at full speed was their headless nightmare. Except, instead of riding on a horse, he was riding in a carriage behind a horse.

The rumble of gigantic wheels mingled with the thunder of hooves, and the sound was deafening.

CHAPTER FOURTEEN

Headless in New York

On top of the crashing hooves, the deafening clatter of carriage wheels rattled across the tarmac, growing louder by the moment. The horseman was holding a pair of leather reins that he furiously slapped against the horse's haunches, causing it to gallop faster and faster until it was practically stomping on top of the frightened teens.

Hammy nearly ran into four garbage cans that lined the trail, hidden in the shadows. At the last second, he veered to the right onto a pedestrian sidewalk. The hurtling vehicle had swerved wildly to the left of the cans and shot past the terrified trio. At that instant, Gwen pointed in Hammy's direction and shouted, "Follow that path through the trees."

Hammy and Leo followed Gwen as she turned onto a narrow footpath that immediately forked in two directions. Without slowing to ponder, Gwen shouted, "Take the left trail."

Once again, Hammy and Leo trailed Gwen without a second thought. Thanks to the garbage cans and Gwen's rapid detour, the Headless Horseman had missed the turnoff and was nowhere in sight. In addition, Hammy noticed the path they were on was too narrow for the huge, white carriage. With formidable green lamp posts on the left side of the trail, and massive trees growing right up to the other side, it would be impossible for the bulky carriage to follow them.

Yet this did not cause Hammy and the twins to slow down as they scurried to put as much distance between themselves and the horseman as they possibly could. They ran on, with Gwen shouting directions whenever they got to a fork in the trail.

Finally, they came to an opening in the trees and saw the eerily glowing skyscrapers of New York City towering on the horizon. Gwen signaled for her companions to stop, and they all bent over with their hands on their knees, gasping for air. Between wheezing breaths, Leo wondered aloud, "Do you think we lost him? There's no way that carriage could have made it this far on that narrow path."

Neither Hammy nor Gwen dared to answer. It seemed that every time they thought they had escaped, they had been wrong.

"He couldn't have followed us in the carriage," Gwen said. "But what's to stop him from getting off and following us on foot?"

Hammy straightened up from his crouched position then let out a gasp. All color drained from his face. "He didn't follow us on foot," he said. His voice carried the heavy weight of fear and defeat.

Both Gwen and Leo hesitated before following Hammy's gaze. Their eyes grew wider than the gigantic lamps glowing down from above. Leo said what they all thought. "Not the horse again." All of his strength left him as he stared at the Headless Horseman who was now mounted on another gigantic steed and cantering toward the three of them.

Leo spoke with a mixture of confusion and terror. "How can that be possible? This guy is like a bad dream that never ends."

Less than twenty yards away, the Headless Horseman sat atop a beastly horse. This time, the steed was dark brown instead of black and was missing a saddle. But it was every bit as gigantic as the horseman's original mount… and even more frightening.

Hammy sprinted away from the mounted terror, needing no encouragement from his companions. The sound of horse's hooves drowned out those of the Skyler twins, who closely trailed their friend. Hammy thought about ducking off the path, but a thick hedge grew alongside the route, a living barrier, impossible to penetrate. With each footstep Hammy carried visions of the marauding horse trampling him under its steely hooves.

The footpath appeared to be leading toward a large pond, overshadowed by buildings that stretched into the sky. The smooth trail curved to the left, and Hammy had trouble following it in the dark. At one point, he careened off an iron fence and nearly tumbled over the top of it.

Rounding the bend at top speed, Hammy could barely make out a stone bridge a few yards in front of him. Both Leo and Gwen caught up, and all three ran side by side until they neared the middle of the bridge where they skidded to a stop and beheld a new haunting vision. On the far side of the bridge was another mounted stranger, this one wearing a gothic top-hat and a leather coat that shone in the diffused lights of a city that never sleeps.

The mounted stranger held up his palm, signalling for them to stop. In the center of the bridge, with nowhere to go, Hammy scanned from the person in front of him to the steep drop-off on either side of the bridge. He continued his gaze back to where he had just come from. On that side of the bridge sat the Headless Horseman, blocking any possibility of escape.

Gwen broke away from Leo and Hammy, then courageously took a couple steps toward the Headless Horseman. In a loud but wavering voice, she demanded, "What do you want? Why are you stalking us?"

Hammy switched his gaze from Gwen to the newly arrived horseman and recognized him as the carriage driver they had spoken with when they first entered the park. One of the eerie park lamps cast its feeble light down onto the man but failed to penetrate the brim of his hat. His face was hidden in the hat's shadow giving him an aura of mystery that caused Hammy to shiver with fear. The fear grew even more ominous as the man and his horse clopped onto the bridge effectively removing any possibility for escape.

Hammy was puzzled when the Headless Horseman reach up toward his hat. Without bothering to answer Gwen's question, he urged his horse toward the middle of the bridge, closing the distance between them and squeezing Hammy and the twins into a tighter and tighter vice.

"I'm not sure I like this," Leo muttered. The other horse rider closed in on the trio. If escaping was ever a choice, that option had disappeared like a ghost in the night.

"What in the..." Gwen uttered, staring at the Headless Horseman who had grasped his hat and appeared to be lifting his entire head off his neck. The strange light still shone down on his jack-o-lantern face as the head rose up and away from the horseman's body. Now he truly would be headless.

A voice came from beneath the rising head. "I can't believe you guys ran all the way into New York City. I started to think I would never catch you."

Gwen fixed her gaze on the Headless Horseman. "And you never will catch us if..." She stopped, mid-sentence and gaped at the figure on the horse.

Hammy and Leo simultaneously stepped toward Gwen, and they formed a tight little knot of bewilderment, momentarily stunned into silence.

Hammy was the first to regain his voice. "Mr. Holland?" He uttered.

The three dumbfounded friends stared at each other and then back at the no-longer-headless horseman. The last person they would have figured to be following them all night long was their sixth grade Language Arts teacher.

"What are you doing here?" Leo asked, with more than a little confusion in his voice.

Mr. Holland waved to the horseman who had been on opposite side of the bridge but was now leading his hefty mount to join the Sleepy Hollow gang. As the strangely dressed fellow drew near, Mr. Holland said, "Thanks Felix. I may have never stopped these three without your help." Mr. Holland introduced the man to Hammy and the twins. "This is Felix. We work together in the summer." He pointed toward the three drowned rats on the bridge. "These are the hooligans I've been chasing all night."

Felix nodded to the teens, then turned to Mr. Holland. "What did you do with the carriage?"

Mr. Holland hitched his thumb in the direction from which he had just ridden. "It's back on Center Drive. When these three detoured onto this path, I knew the carriage would be too wide to follow, so I unhitched it from the horse. I didn't know if old Mr. Ned," he reached down to pet the horse's neck, "would let me ride him. But he was fine with it."

"We've met him before," Leo said, remembering Felix as the carriage driver they had first spoken to when they ventured into the park.

"Why did you chase us here?" Gwen blurted, expressing a mixture of embarrassment and anger.

"We don't have time for that now," Mr. Holland said. "We need to return Mr. Ned to his carriage and then hustle to Grand Central Station. The last train for Tarrytown leaves at ten minutes before midnight.'

Felix jumped into the conversation. "You'll never make it unless you get going now. I'll take care of the horses. You need to find a taxi."

"I'll at least take Mr. Ned back to the carriage. Then I'll take you up on your offer, but I owe you, big time."

"We're in agreement on that point. At the very least, I'd say you'll be buying me breakfast every day next summer."

Mr. Holland led the way on his horse, followed by the three runaways. Felix followed closely behind them on his horse as they all hustled along the lamplit trail back to where Hammy had collided with the garbage cans.

Once they got back to the abandoned carriage, Mr. Holland tied his horse up to a sign-post, shook hands with Felix, then herded his students down the nearly deserted Center Drive. "We'll have plenty of time to talk once we're on the train."

As soon as they emerged from the park, they crossed a busy street, and Mr. Holland hailed a yellow taxi. He instructed the driver that they were going to Grand Central Station. Riding in a taxi was the latest in a long string of new adventures for the Skyler twins that evening.

Mr. Holland sat in the front seat across from the driver, while Hammy and the twins climbed into the back seat. For the first couple minutes, the taxi was silent while everyone caught their breath and tried to sort through the crazy events of the day. If the night had been a dream, it had been extremely realistic and more than just a little bizarre.

CHAPTER FIFTEEN

Back to the Hollow

It wasn't a dream. Mr. Holland turned around in his seat and studied the sheepish-looking hoodlums in the back. His face became serious for a moment, then the old Mr. Holland's smile reappeared. "You three are hard to keep track of. What made you decide to come to New York City?"

Hammy explained about the unexpected express train until Gwen chimed in. "Why were you on a horse and wearing a bizarre costume? And what were you doing in the cemetery?"

Before Mr. Holland could reply, the taxi pulled up to Grand Central Station. Hammy and the twins climbed out of the cab and waited for their teacher while he paid for the taxi ride. As soon as he got out of the car, he hurried everyone into the station and toward the center of the cavernous main hall, where the golden, four-sided clock showed that it was 11:45.

Mr. Holland studied the lighted train schedule board on the wall nearby. "We need to hurry. We can buy our tickets on the train. I know I always tell you guys not to run in the halls, but you're going to have to ignore that now or we won't make it."

The four of them sprinted through the station with Mr. Holland leading the way. He often checked to make sure Hammy kept up, but he never slowed down. Soon they entered a narrow tunnel that emptied onto a larger train platform. A conductor appeared in the open door of one of the train cars.

"Quick," Mr. Holland shouted, loud enough for the students and the conductor to hear him.

They stepped onto the train just as the doors were closing. Mr. Holland had to block the sliding door as it nearly hissed shut in Hammy's face. It slid back open as Hammy jumped aboard. The conductor shot an irritated gaze at Mr. Holland and an even angrier one at the three youths.

"Sorry," Mr. Holland said to the conductor. "I was horsing around in the park for a little too long."

Hammy laughed, appreciating Mr. Holland's familiar classroom humor. For the first time that evening, Hammy was hopeful that everything might still turn out okay. Yet he still had a hollow sensation in the pit of his stomach when he thought about his parents and the missing *Sleepy Hollow* book.

Quite a few people were scattered throughout the train car with the bulk of them sitting on the left side, where they would enjoy a view over the Hudson River throughout their ride. Mr. Holland led the way toward the center of the car and found an empty row of seats, spacious enough for all four of them. As soon as they sat down, Mr. Holland pulled out his phone and began pecking away. Hammy had a dozen questions, but he knew better than to interrupt what appeared to be important business.

The train lurched forward and plunged into the dark underbelly of New York City. Both of the twins yawned, and their heads lurched back and forth with the rhythm of the train. Mr. Holland finished typing on his phone and stuck it back in his pocket. Hammy began to ask his first question, but he was interrupted again by the conductor collecting tickets and fares. Mr. Holland paid the fare for all four of them.

"We'll pay you back as soon as we get home," Leo said.

"You mean your parents will pay me back."

Once the conductor completed his business and moved on, Gwen repeated the question she had asked earlier. "You still haven't told us why you wore a Headless Horseman costume and rode a horse into the Sleepy Hollow Cemetery?"

Mr. Holland smiled. "I guess I could ask you three what you were doing sitting on the Bronze Lady statue in the cemetery on Halloween night, but I already know the answer to that question."

All three of the teens exchanged glances, then peered over at Mr. Holland with puzzled expressions on their faces. He continued. "I overheard part of your conversation with James and Ely in the hall outside my classroom earlier today. It sounded like they were blackmailing you into going to the cemetery tonight. So I thought I'd check up on you."

"But that doesn't really answer why you were on a horse and dressed like the Headless Horseman." Gwen was persistent, bordering on rude.

"I'm getting to that part," Mr. Holland continued. "I was in the Sleepy Hollow Halloween Parade. That's why I said I hoped I'd see you all there during class today. The Purcell family lets me ride their horses on weekends, and they loaned me one for the parade. Aren't you guys friends with Randy and Tammy Purcell?"

Hammy and Leo nodded their heads. Gwen grunted, then continued her interrogation. "What did you do with the horse when you got on the train?"

"I tied it up at the station and called the Purcells as soon as I was on board. They were still downtown with their horse trailers since the twins also rode in the parade, so they said they could pick up the horse."

"What I don't get," Leo said, "is why you kept your mask on that whole time."

Mr. Holland smiled. "I didn't keep it on the whole time. I took it off while riding the train. But in case you didn't notice, it's been raining most of the evening." He held up the mask. "The hat and mask are all one piece, so if I put the hat on, I also put the mask on. I wore the hat for the same reason the three of you wore hoods and hats tonight."

"I still got sopping wet," Hammy said. "I wish we had an umbrella."

"Thanks for trying to help us, Mr. Holland," Leo said. "I hate to ask another favor, but could we use your phone to call our parents? They're probably really mad at us about now."

"I've been in touch with them all night long, so they're familiar with what's going on," Mr. Holland replied. "I texted them right after we got on the train. They'll be waiting at the station when we arrive."

"I'm going to be in huge trouble," Hammy moaned.

"I told them the whole story about James and Ely. I can't guarantee anything, but they shouldn't be too mad," Mr. Holland reassured them. "And they know that the Headless Horseman chased you through town and onto the train. I think they'll have some questions for you about your trip to New York City though."

Hammy's face became even more drawn. "Speaking of James and Ely, did my dad say anything about the *Legend of Sleepy Hollow* book?

He's not going to be any too happy about that."

"I almost forgot," Mr. Holland said, as he reached into his long, black cloak and unzipped an inner pocket. "I have something for all three of you." He pulled out three cell phones and handed them to Hammy and the twins. "After you guys hightailed it out of the cemetery, I ran into a couple of your friends. They were hanging onto these for you."

"Wait," Gwen interrupted. "You saw James and Ely? What did they say? Did you push them over the bridge for us? Please say you did."

Mr. Holland tried hard to launch a stern gaze in Gwen's direction, but he missed the mark. "No I didn't push them over the bridge, but I doubt they'll be bothering you anytime soon. A certain Headless Horseman had a serious conversation with them, and they looked almost ready to jump over the bridge on their own."

Mr. Holland turned to face Hammy. "And I got one more thing from them." He reached back into his black cloak and pulled out a familiar book. "I believe you've been looking for this." He handed the well-worn novel to Hammy. Other than being a bit soggy, it appeared to be in better shape than he thought it would be.

Hammy looked as if he was about to start weeping. "Thank you Mr. Holland. If you weren't my teacher, I'd hug you."

"Well I am your teacher." He looked out the window as the train began to slow down. "And we're almost to Tarrytown, so get ready to go." He pointed toward the exit door.

Hammy also glanced out the train window just as they pulled into the Tarrytown station. The platform, typically bustling with waiting passengers, appeared desolate with the exception of four worried-looking parents trying to peer inside each train car, hoping for a glimpse of their children.

"They don't seem too mad," Gwen said. The four city travelers stood and made their way to the exit.

As soon as they disembarked from the train, they were besieged by relieved parents who alternated between hugging their children and thanking Mr. Holland. Hammy sheepishly handed the Sleepy Hollow book to his father, who didn't even seem to notice the sogginess.

Hammy cast a lusty glance at the closed train station bakery as they passed by. He decided it might not be a the best idea to ask about coming back for breakfast. Maybe he could suggest it in the morning.

Gwen was less reluctant to speak. "Maybe we can do this again next Halloween."

For a change, Gwen was on the receiving end of some nasty glares and rude comments.